Bloom's
GUIDES

Charles Dickens's

A Christmas Carol

CURRENTLY AVAILABLE

The Adventures of Huckleberry Finn
The Adventures of Tom Sawyer
All Quiet on the Western Front
Animal Farm
The Autobiography of Malcolm X
The Awakening
The Bell Jar
Beloved
Beowulf
Black Boy
The Bluest Eye
Brave New World
The Canterbury Tales
Catch-22
The Catcher in the Rye
The Chosen
A Christmas Carol
The Crucible
Cry, the Beloved Country
Death of a Salesman
Fahrenheit 451
A Farewell to Arms
Frankenstein
The Glass Menagerie
The Grapes of Wrath
Great Expectations
The Great Gatsby
The Handmaid's Tale
Heart of Darkness
The Hobbit
The House on Mango Street
I Know Why the Caged Bird Sings
The Iliad
Invisible Man
Jane Eyre
The Joy Luck Club
The Kite Runner
Lord of the Flies
Macbeth
Maggie: A Girl of the Streets
The Metamorphosis
Native Son
Night
1984
The Odyssey
Oedipus Rex
Of Mice and Men
One Hundred Years of Solitude
Pride and Prejudice
Ragtime
A Raisin in the Sun
The Red Badge of Courage
The Road
Romeo and Juliet
The Scarlet Letter
A Separate Peace
Slaughterhouse-Five
The Stranger
A Streetcar Named Desire
The Sun Also Rises
A Tale of Two Cities
Their Eyes Were Watching God
To Kill a Mockingbird
Uncle Tom's Cabin
The Waste Land
Wuthering Heights

Bloom's

GUIDES

Charles Dickens's

A Christmas Carol

Edited & with an Introduction
by Harold Bloom

BLOOM'S LITERARY CRITICISM
An Infobase Learning Company

Bloom's Guides: A Christmas Carol

Bloom's Literary Criticism
An imprint of Infobase Learning
132 West 31st Street
New York NY 10001

Library of Congress Cataloging-in-Publication Data
Charles Dickens's A Christmas carol / edited and with an introduction by Harold Bloom.
p. cm. — (Bloom's guides)
Includes bibliographical references and index.
ISBN 978-1-61753-001-2 (hardcover : acid-free paper)
1. Dickens, Charles, 1812–1870. Christmas carol. I. Bloom, Harold. II. Title: A Christmas carol.
PR4572.C683C47 2011
823'.8—dc22
2011017001

Bloom's Literary Criticism books are available at special discounts when purchased in bulk quantities for businesses, associations, institutions, or sales promotions. Please call our Special Sales Department in New York at (212) 967–8800 or (800) 322–8755.

You can find Bloom's Literary Criticism on the World Wide Web at http://www.infobaselearning.com

Contributing editor: Portia Williams Weiskel
Cover designed by Takeshi Takahashi
Composition by IBT Global, Troy NY
Cover printed by Yurchak Printing, Landisville PA
Book printed and bound by Yurchak Printing, Landisville PA
Date printed: June 2011
Printed in the United States of America

10 9 8 7 6 5 4 3 2 1

This book is printed on acid-free paper.

Contents

Introduction

HAROLD BLOOM

After Shakespeare, Charles Dickens is the writer in English whose effect on the world's readers transcends the apparent limits of literature and so teaches us that imaginative invention itself can be a form of life. Together with *The Pickwick Papers*, *A Christmas Carol* seems as though it has always been there, just as Hamlet and Falstaff give us the strong illusion they did not require Shakespeare's art to have awarded them life.

Mr. Pickwick and Ebenezer Scrooge are myths, ageless and universal, and their tales edge on dimensions that waver between cautionary fables and spiritual verities. The lovable founder of the Pickwick Club is of a greater aesthetic eminence than Scrooge, yet everyone knows the name and miserliness of Scrooge, while Pickwick is now an elitist taste.

A Christmas Carol in Prose: Being a Ghost Story of Christmas is a narrative of about 30,000 words yet seems shorter to me each time I reread it. The Christmas season of the United States essentially was inaugurated by this most popular of all Dickens's works.

Like Chaucer, Dickens wrote in order to read aloud to an audience, and *A Christmas Carol* became the greatest success of all his public performances. The oral style superbly heightens the gusto with which Scrooge is represented:

> Oh! But he was a tight-fisted hand at the grindstone, Scrooge! a squeezing, wrenching, grasping, scraping, clutching, covetous, old sinner! Hard and sharp as flint, from which no steel had ever struck out generous fire; secret, and self-contained, and solitary as an oyster. The cold within him froze his old features, nipped his pointed nose, shrivelled his cheek, stiffened his gait; made his eyes red, his thin lips blue; and spoke out shrewdly in his grating voice. A frosty rime was on his head, and on

> his eyebrows, and his wiry chin. He carried his own low temperature always about with him; he iced his office in the dog-days; and didn't thaw it one degree at Christmas.

Magnificently vivid, this style carries an undersong of what we frequently value in "children's literature" and in early romance: a closeness to origins by which we find our way back to a primal exuberance. Scrooge is a negative sublime in himself, and inevitably he is open to hauntings by ghosts. After Scrooge himself and Tiny Tim, we remember *A Christmas Carol* for its spooks: Marley's Ghost, and the Three Spirits—the ghosts of Christmas Past, Christmas Present, Christmas Yet to Come.

We delight in Dickens's ghosts and goblins because they are lively and make our flesh crawl. And yet their triumphant excess inspired Franz Kafka into his own surpassing uncanniness. They testify to an otherness that emphasizes their author's deep affinities with the Shakespeare of *Macbeth*.

Scrooge's total conversion persuades us precisely because he is a myth, both more and less than a man. So fiercely splendid was the miserly Scrooge that aesthetically I lament his apotheosis as a benign force for generosity and good. But that is the sorrow of myth: We want Scrooge to be Scrooge just as we wish no reform to engulf Fagin or Uriah Heep. Belated benevolence is not the aim of art: Let Iago be Iago and give us woe or wonder. The comic genius of Dickens celebrated the grotesque but withdrew from the darker consequences of loss. Perhaps *The Christmas Carol* someday will seem only a period piece, yet its time has not yet passed.

Biographical Sketch

A chronological accounting of the life and work of a major cultural figure such as Charles Dickens provides historical context and reliable dates and details but is less interesting than commentary and analysis that includes informed speculation and attempts at psychological insight. This observation has particular relevance for understanding Dickens's life because for decades the only source of biographical material was to be found in the memoirlike biography published by John Forster in 1872–74, two years after Dickens's death in 1870. Forster was both a friend and contemporary of Dickens and was excited, challenged, and honored when asked to be the author's biographer. As Grahame Smith points out in his essay "The Life and Times of Charles Dickens," Forster—as friend and confidant—had reason to shape the work in a way favorable to Dickens and intentionally omitted information that—if made public—would have been awkward for Dickens (see *Cambridge Companion*, 1–15). Important examples of omitted material include Dickens's choice to keep undisclosed even from his family his harsh experiences as a child laborer and his involvement in later life with a woman not his wife. A standard biography did not appear until Edgar Johnson's two-volume *Charles Dickens: His Tragedy and Triumph* (1952). More substantial biographies are now available.

A notable feature of Dickens's earliest years were their instability. Frequent reversals in economic circumstances forced the family to move from place to place, each move bringing disruption and change—at times to pleasant and nurturing surroundings but also to situations that made for anxiety and limitation. Having to adjust to new and contrasting conditions possibly contributed to the reputation Dickens acquired over his lifetime as being a writer who was able to give sympathetic and dramatic portrayal of life at all levels of the English class structure.

Dickens was born on February 7, 1812, in the Portsmouth area of England, where his father, John Dickens, was employed as a clerk in the navy pay office. It was a center of much commercial and political activity because of England's wars against Napoleon and the United States. Dickens, known as Charley to his family, was one of six children. The most difficult period of family life stemmed from the father's ill handling of his earnings, leading finally, in 1824, to serious debt. It was a period in English history, according to critic Les Standiford, "when it was the custom to treat a debtor little differently from a man who had reached into a purse and stolen a similar sum" (*The Man Who Invented Christmas*, 2). With a debt of 40 pounds, John Dickens was taken to a form of detention center and given a limited period of time to appeal to friends and family for the necessary funds. When the rescue failed to materialize, Charles had to witness his father being taken to Marshalsea, a debtor's prison, and, as a consequence, the rest of his family descend into poverty and shame. To help support the family, he was required to leave school and work as a laborer.

Dickens's experience at Warren's Blacking Factory has generated a range of commentary. There is no disputing that, because of his father's debt, twelve-year-old Dickens worked ten-hour days under dark, unpleasant, and sometimes cold conditions filling small pots with shoe blacking and pasting a printed label on each, earning six shillings per week. It is easy to imagine—and Dickens much later revealed these feelings—that both physically and emotionally the experience was a nightmare. About the age of 47, just before publishing *David Copperfield* (1849–50), he wrote about the factory with " . . . its rotten floors and staircase, and the old grey rats swarming down in the cellars, and the sound of their squeaking and scuffling coming up the stairs at all times, and the dirt and decay of the place" (quoted in *The Man Who Invented Christmas*, 3).

Some critics point out that Dickens spent only six months in the factory and perhaps exaggerated its unpleasantness to gain public sympathy, but that theory would fail to explain why Dickens chose to keep this period of his life hidden until much later. American writer Edmund Wilson was among the first of Dickens's critics to contextualize the experience; he reminded readers that Dickens was forced to leave the school he was enjoying, endure the shame of his father's imprisonment and his family's struggles, and live with the sense of betrayal that his mother would permit such a fate to befall him. Wilson writes:

> These experiences produced in Charles Dickens a trauma from which he suffered all his life. . . . For the adult in desperate straits, it is almost always possible to imagine, if not to contrive, some way out; for the child, for whom love and freedom have inexplicably been taken away, no relief or release can be projected. (*Triple Thinkers: Wound and Bow*, 7)

Readers of Dickens's novels are familiar with his frequent references to factory work and the grim images associated with it, most vividly in *David Copperfield.* His fiction also contains many sympathetic portrayals of neglected and orphaned children who find themselves in unjust, frightening, and impoverishing circumstances, as well as portrayals of people suffering under different conditions of literal and emotional imprisonment.

Although Dickens never received a university education, he mentions several happy and successful early experiences of being in school. In London and Chatham, he attended primary schools and produced at age nine a work called *Misnar, the Sultan of India.* When his father was released from prison after receiving a small inheritance, Dickens was able to leave the factory job and attend a boarding school, where he spent two happy and productive years. The writer and Catholic apologist G.K. Chesterton points out in his admiring study of Dickens that John Dickens—even after returning to gainful employment—failed to provide for his son's advanced education. Apparently, however, he took pleasure in his son's enthusiasm and talent for learning and encouraged Charles to perform little skits and stories for the family's entertainment—an identity and pastime Dickens continued to the end of his life.

In the first chapter of her book, *Knowing Dickens* (2007), Rosemarie Bodenheimer counters claims made by some of Dickens's contemporaries that his lack of formal education reduced his storytelling skills to something more like eccentricity than genius. She looks at other resources Dickens made use of for his self-structured education, including frequent visits to museums and the theater and voracious reading. Dickens acquired a substantial library of English and American literature and on his two trips to the United States became acquainted with history and biography. Natural history also interested him—Darwin's work was in his library—as did psychic phenomena such as "twilight" states of consciousness, although he was adamantly skeptical about séances and other displays of communicating with the dead. Dickens also taught himself all the current theories concerning the brain and the practice of mesmerism.

Dickens is given credit for publishing's rise in popularity because of his prolific offerings and for their accessibility to the public. He began his long career in 1833 when he published his first story, "A Dinner at Poplar Walk," and became a reporter for *The Morning Chronicle*. The next decade was especially productive. He married Catherine Hogarth in 1834 and six of his ten children were born to her. Dickens drew popular attention to himself immediately after he began writing his stories and sketches about London street life. First published anonymously and then by the penname Boz, his stories were solicited by several London publications. In 1836, two sets of stories—both called *Sketches by Boz*—were published under his name, and he was at work on *Pickwick Papers*.

In 1837, Dickens began his long and lucrative tradition of serializing his publications, beginning with *Pickwick Papers* and *Oliver Twist*. He and his various editors worked out a system of publishing a novel in sections, each selling for a shilling, each with the additional appeal of having solicited illustrations to accompany the text. After the series was complete, the publisher would bring out the whole work in a single volume selling for up to 21 shillings. Although no records of literacy rates existed in England at that time, an estimation of somewhere between 300,000 and 500,000 readers (in a total population of two million people) has been estimated (see Standiford, 29). Using records of Dickens's sales, it appears that he was being read by one-fifth to one-quarter of England's population.

Successfully producing popular and affordable literature served the commercial purposes of both Dickens and his publishers and, most notably, satisfied the author's sense of himself as a writer for all classes of English society. One feature of serialized storytelling that turned out to have populist implications was the opportunity it gave to readers and friends to wield influence over a story's outcome. Anyone so inclined could exert pressure on the author before the next installment was published. In one instance, a reader recognized herself in a character from *David Copperfield* and persuaded Dickens to recast this character in a more positive light.

Dickens made two trips to the United States, the first in 1842 and the second, arranged as a public reading tour, in 1867. He also brought his family to live in Italy for a year and to Paris for several months. There were moves as well within London; these ended when the successful author was able to purchase a home at Gad's Hill Place, a site near Rochester in Kent that he had admired from a distance since his early years. An early (but disappointing) foray into acting and the theater was revived in 1857 when he took a role in and directed a play, *The Frozen Deep*. In this new circle of friends, he met and fell in love with a young actress, which led to his separation from his wife a year later.

Dickens's Christian roots are well known. Critic Valentine Cunningham writes: "[He was a] very English, Protestant, and Anglican-inflected [Christian writer]" ("Dickens and Christianity," *Companion*, 255). Baptized in the Church of England, he attended sermons in different churches every Sunday and went to chapel services in the evening. His religious ideas took a liberal bent, and his church affiliations were eclectic. During his first trip to the United States, he was inspired by the preaching of William Ellery Channing, the fiery Unitarian minister known for his passionate opposition to slavery. In a letter to a friend, Dickens spoke of joining the Unitarian Church in part because Unitarians "[*would*] do something for human improvement . . . [and practiced] Charity and Toleration" (ibid, 259). This influence shows up in the many phrases used in the titles given to critical commentary about Dickens's work—such terms as *social gospel, moral imperatives,* and *class consciousness. A Christmas Carol* (1843) is explicitly about the importance of religious conversion for the development of compassion leading to the enactment of social justice legislation for, especially, the poor and working classes in English society.

Dickens also became a famous and beloved public performer of his own stories. His readings of *A Christmas Carol* were the most numerous and the most popular. His American reading tour (an inspired Mark Twain attended one of these performances in New York) was enthusiastically received but left him physically weakened. In April 1869, he began his Farewell Reading Tour in Leeds. Public performances had become his favorite activity and he continued to put great emotion into each reading—so much so that friends and family members worried that he would become physically ill if he continued to exert himself in this way. In his study of Dickens as a public performer, Malcolm Andrews quotes from a report given by a woman in a Boston audience who was distressed while watching Dickens approach the lectern to begin one of his last readings: "[H]e appeared to be very lame . . . unable to walk alone [but when he appeared before the crowd he was transformed, able] to walk erect . . . with his accustomed ease and grace of deportment [until the end when he evinced] great pain and weariness . . . out of sight of the audience" (*Charles Dickens and His Performing Selves,* 263–64). A series of small strokes around the same time likely weakened him as well; his son recalled performances when he was unable to pronounce *Pickwick,* coming up instead with *Picksnick, Picnic,* and *Peckwicks* (ibid, 264).

Dickens's doctor was summoned following one of these impaired performances, and afterward the author was persuaded to announce that he would give his final readings at St. James Hall in London. On March 15, 1870, as he began this final performance, the 2,000-member audience rose and cheered him for several minutes. He chose his favorite—*A Christmas Carol*—for his final performance. Called back several times with applause at the conclusion, Dickens made an emotional announcement of his retirement from the stage: " . . .

from these garish lights I vanish now for evermore," the words used twelve weeks later to inscribe the funeral card for his burial in the Poets' Corner of Westminster Abbey on June 14, following his death on June 9, 1870.

Accounts of Dickens's funeral include scenes of thousands of mourners visiting the author's grave every day for months, leaving flowers and other tokens of devotion. In its obituary, the *London Times* (June 10, 1870) noted that Dickens "[had become] the intimate of every household [and his death] will be felt by millions as nothing less than a personal bereavement" (reprinted in *Charles Dickens: The Critical Heritage*, Philip Collins, ed., 1971, 506).

Dickens was an "intimate" presence in each household not only because he was so widely and warmly read but also because he seemed able to see deeply inside people's lives and minds. Scholars often comment that Dickens's work is in part an encyclopedia of Victorian social life, documenting in the stories innumerable details about household life and relationships, class-based customs, street life, and legal and commercial issues. Edmund Wilson must have had a similar appreciation of Dickens when, more than a half century after the *Times* obituary, he lamented that the author's reputation had fluctuated in the interim and urged that Dickens be allowed " . . . to exorcise the spell which has bewitched him into a stuffy piece of household furniture and [to be granted] his proper rank as the poet of that portièred and upholstered world who saw clearest through the covering and the curtains (*Wound and Bow*, 9–10).

The Story Behind the Story

In his preface to *The Cambridge Companion to Charles Dickens*, John O. Jordan writes: "In North America . . . *A Christmas Carol* has attained virtually the status of myth and elicits parodies, piracies, and annual theatrical performances with increasing frequency" (xix). Students of Dickens's life will discover many references linking him with the celebration of Christmas, even crediting him with the revival of its English and American versions. There are several accounts of an incident in which a woman was overheard exclaiming on the day that Dickens died, June 9, 1870, "Dickens dead? Then will Father Christmas die too?" (Davis 53).

Dickens, of course, did not invent Christmas, but he successfully reintegrated earlier traditions and memories of traditions and, in effect, repurposed the Christmas season. Three unrelated historical circumstances overlapped to bring about this cultural phenomenon. In 1843, the year *A Christmas Carol* was written and published, Dickens was at a low point of his personal history. His popularity as a writer and his income—both recently quite substantial—had fallen with the disappointing sales of *Martin Chuzzlewit.* Dickens was ready to leave fiction and rely instead on travel writing, which, following his trip to the United States, had brought him some success. Had other factors not been present, *A Christmas Carol* and most of the author's other best-loved stories might never have been written.

Social and economic conditions of this period of English history also played a part. The Industrial Revolution had changed both the English landscape and the relationships among laborers and landowners. The decade before *A Christmas Carol* appeared was full of political and social tension, culminating in often violent strikes by miners and spinners, the hanging of nine agricultural workers, and the destruction of farm fields and equipment. Pam Morris, in her discussion of the influence of this period on Dickens (*Dickens's Class Consciousness*, 1991), reminds readers that political tensions were exacerbated by the specter of the French Revolution a century earlier, which raised fears in the English upper classes about strikes and rebellions fomented by the lower classes.

As a writer known for his sympathies for people of all classes and, in particular, for children in downtrodden and abusive circumstances, Dickens felt himself under personal and public pressure to promote efforts to educate homeless and neglected children and to support the legislative proposals of the Factory Movement—a contemporary political effort to ameliorate or eliminate child labor and other practices that added misery to the already disadvantaged working classes. Dickens's eventual involvement was not the direct action his reputation for compassion for these issues would have suggested. He certainly knew the radical writings of Karl Marx and Friedrich Engel about the mistreatment of the working classes but would have resisted a complete overthrow of capitalism.

There is persuasive evidence to support some scholarly speculation (see, for example, Vogel, pp. 57–68) that instead of direct political involvement, Dickens put his compassion (and perhaps guilt) concerning unjust and inhumane treatment of the lower social classes into writing his story about a miser and a desperately poor family. *A Christmas Carol* brought into focus an age-old paradox about inequities among the social classes and the social imperatives contained in the biblical story of Christmas. Dickens scholar Joseph W. Childers writes:

> We can . . . see . . . in *A Christmas Carol* . . . how Christmas struggles against competing views of social responsibility that are likewise attempting to resolve the contradictions of the Victorian everyday in the 1840s. [It takes up] the issue of the poor, the other nation, and the increasing gap between the lower and upper classes . . . in *A Christmas Carol* we are told explicitly that it is the job of Christmas to heal, at least temporarily, the breach between humans that has come about as a result of modern modes of producing and modern ways of doing business. ("So, This Is Christmas," *Contemporary Dickens*, 117–18)

It is not surprising—given Dickens's gift for storytelling, his current financial predicament, and the contentious social and political issues pressing on him—that the idea of writing something like *A Christmas Carol* would come to him, but, according to letters exchanged with John Forster, the idea for the work came suddenly and almost rapturously. Following an address he had just given at the Athenaeum in Manchester about the importance of education for all classes, he was back in London walking the streets, recalling with great satisfaction the rapport he had established with the audience on that evening. The prospect of writing another story for this audience—a story that both portrayed the plight of the English poor and offered a profound and spiritual solution for the country's economic disparities—was deeply satisfying. Bit by bit the story came together, and Dickens described to his biographer how he was moved both to tears and laughter at his new prospect. (See Standiford, *The Man Who Invented Christmas*, 44–70.) A third part of the story of Dickens and Christmas was the status of Christmas itself at the time. Christmas—the ecclesiastical celebration of the birth of Jesus—is hundreds of years old, but its popular observances have undergone many changes. One year before *Carol* was published (1843), for example, there was no custom of exchanging Christmas cards, nor anything like a written Christmas greeting. The first one appeared the same year as *Carol* and depicted a festive scene harking back to the Christmas revelers in medieval England. Its images of feasting and decorative greenery, however, are more recognizable to contemporary celebrators of Christmas than those in 1843. (For a fuller discussion of the evolution of Christmas in England and *Carol*'s influence, see Paul Davis, *The Lives and Times of Ebenezer Scrooge*.)

The relatively spare version of Christmas observances at the time was partly due to the expanding division of the population—due to England's industrialization—into urban and rural dwellers. Those who fled the countryside seeking work in the city often left behind their traditions and parts of their extended families. Family members who would have gathered to celebrate were now too far away from one another to reasonably do so. Calvinist Puritanism, another influence, opposed the celebration of Christmas. "Whether lost on the exodus into the new towns or stifled by the smothering hand of Calvinism, the old English Christmas was largely a memory by the beginning of the nineteenth century" (Davis 19).

The memories, however, were kept alive in the popular imagination by various publications—Robert Seymour's *Book of Christmas* (1837) is an example—that recorded for nostalgic purposes images and ideas from an earlier time in history. Davis includes a print of a painting from 1838 of a medieval Christmas celebration (*Merry Christmas in the Baron's Hall*, 21) depicting elaborate festivities being enjoyed by members of the baronial family in the company of members of the servant class along with random townspeople—all united in a common celebration rather than divided by social class in separate observances. This blending of all members of the English population appealed to Dickens and served his desire to be known as a writer for all classes of people.

In this convergence of influences, *A Christmas Carol* was written and published.

Coming onto the market just before Christmas 1843 and designed with a red-and-gold cover to appear enticingly festive, the book was an instant success, selling out its first run of 6,000 copies in a few days. Its social message was a plea to its English readers to develop a social conscience through opening their hearts to the plight of others and sharing the collective wealth. Its promise was that such a gesture would connect readers to the real source of human happiness that comes from leading less selfish lives. The message reconnected with the biblical Christian teachings and together became the foundation for a revival of the English celebration of Christmas. So successfully was this message conveyed that it became part of the English national identity. Citing Dickens's rejuvenation of Christmas, Chesterton writes:

> . . . he was fighting for the old European festival, Pagan and Christian, for that trinity of eating, drinking and praying . . . [and] for the character of Christmas . . . [that] lies chiefly in two things: first on the terrestrial side the note of comfort rather than the note of brightness;

> and on the spiritual side, Christian charity rather than Christian ecstasy. And comfort is, like charity, a very English instinct. (116, 118)

Many Western readers today inherited and carry on these traditions in ways that continue to evolve.

A Christmas Carol is the first of five Christmas books Dickens published between 1843 and 1848. *The Chimes*, *A Cricket on the Hearth*, *The Battle of Life*, and *The Haunted Man* are the others. The tradition of public readings of *A Christmas Carol* that Dickens initiated is almost as popular as the story itself. He believed that reading aloud created a valuable intimacy between a writer and his audience. This rapport was a social good as well. He emphasized how important it was to bring together people from all social classes in a spirit of goodwill. And, whenever he could, he insisted that there would always be seats selling for a single shilling at each performance.

An example of Dickens's success as a performer is found in this review of an 1858 reading of *Carol*: "Mr. Dickens is performing a good service by his readings, diffusing sentiments of kindliness and benevolence amongst all classes, whilst he affords entertainment in a most unexceptional manner" (quoted in Malcolm Andrews, *Charles Dickens and His Performing Selves*, 48). An example of *Carol*'s power is the story of a factory owner in a Boston audience who closed down the factory on Christmas Day and gave each worker a Christmas turkey (see *Christmas Books*, Glancy, ed., xiii).

The performances were also popular because Dickens put so much physical energy into the readings. Many reports exist revealing how he made happy smacking sounds as he pretended to taste the applesauce at the feast and how he used a knife and his fingers to illustrate Mr. Fezziwig's famous dancing trick. After one of his readings, he remarked, "The town was drunk with the *Carol* far into the night" (see *Performing Selves*, 193, 236). There is even a report of chickens getting into the act after the lights coming on for the performance convinced a flock roosting in a nearby rafter to think it was dawn and time to begin crowing (ibid, 146).

A Christmas Carol was and certainly remains popular, but it has not generated much critical commentary, likely because its themes are both old and accessible. It is also a short work of fewer than 30,000 words. (Some interesting recent criticism has appeared dealing with ambiguity in the story's message about the relation between Christmas charity and capitalism. See especially the essay by Childers in *Contemporary Dickens*.) What has been generated by *Carol* is hundreds of adaptations, so many that no accurate record exists, only partial listings. There are also so many variations of the story that scholars such as Paul Davis have to distinguish between the *Carol* (Dickens's published story) and the Carol (remembered versions and references). In addition, the figure of Ebenezer Scrooge belongs to popular culture and has been used in many serious and amusing contexts. Paul Davis has a whole chapter devoted to examples. One is an account of a political controversy brought on in 1983 when Republican White House adviser Edwin Meese challenged the assertion by Democrats that there were hungry children in the United States. He claimed that people joined food lines at soup kitchens because the food was free and they were too lazy to work to afford food for themselves and family members. The Massachusetts Democratic speaker of the house rebutted his claims, referring to him as "a Scrooge at Christmas time" (Davis 221). Another example is the claim made by Jeffrey St. John of the right-leaning John Birch Society that Dickens's *A Christmas Carol* was a textbook of "welfare-state liberalism." According to Davis, St. John found Dickens to be "in league with Franklin Roosevelt [intent on leading] Anglo-American culture down the path of delusion by denouncing 'the business class as composed of heartless and cruel people'" (Davis 223).

It has been observed many times that innumerable people who cannot read and innumerable others who do not read are familiar with and still influenced by Dickens's *A Christmas Carol*. Dickens thought of it as a Christmas present to his country, and Dickens's contemporary William Thackeray called it "a national benefit, and to every man and woman who reads it a personal kindness" (*Fraser's Magazine* 29, February 1844, 169; see Davis, 9).

List of Characters

The character of **Ebenezer Scrooge** has two personalities. Pre-conversion, he is the literary embodiment of miserliness, portrayed as bony and rigid, humorless, and utterly self-absorbed. His mean-spirited instincts repel most of his acquaintances. Dickens describes him as being as "solitary as an oyster." As a miser, he brings suffering to others, but he is also miserable just being himself. The post-conversion Scrooge is a mirror image of his former self: He is capable of compassion and generosity, he seeks rather than repels company, his rigidity gives way to a lively and harmless loss of self-control, and he expels peals of laughter instead of growls.

Jacob Marley was Scrooge's business partner who died seven years before the story begins. His living presence takes a ghostly and ghastly form on Christmas Eve as Scrooge is retiring for the night. As he lived in life, so does he live in death; he was as miserly as Scrooge and as self-absorbed, and he finds himself imprisoned after death, held by the chains that represent his spiritual blindness. Marley's conversion from being dead in life to being alive in death enables Scrooge to realize the error of his ways and carries an implicit belief in the power of free will to change one's life while there is still time. One wonders if Dickens thought of Marley as the Old Testament Jacob providing a ladder to his old partner to help him escape from his spiritual prison.

Fred is Scrooge's too merry nephew; his insistence on celebrating Christmas elicits his uncle's first utterance of "Bah! Humbug!" Fred's mother was Scrooge's sister; Fred has some of her sweetness, which is evident at the end of the story in his offer of comfort and assistance to the Cratchit family. Fred's good-spirited insistence on keeping faith in his uncle's ability to change his mind turns out to be an important factor in Scrooge's conversion.

Bob Cratchit, Scrooge's clerk, is forced to warm himself on a cold day with a single piece of coal begrudgingly given by Scrooge. Cratchit is the father of a large family that includes his physically impaired son, Tiny Tim. Cratchit exemplifies paternal devotion under trying circumstances. He is given a well-deserved raise by post-conversion Scrooge.

The Ghost of Christmas Past has the appearance of both a child and an old man, suggesting the arc of memory one must travel to activate the insights necessary for transformation. During the "trips" back to his past, the ghost appears to mock Scrooge by taking on some of the miser's old attitudes and using his very words in an effort to stimulate him toward a different way of thinking. At the scene of Fezziwig's grand party, for example, the ghost pretends to ridicule the host for spending too much money just to allow others to enjoy themselves.

Mr. Fezziwig, the good-natured owner of the warehouse where Scrooge is apprenticed, is (along with his wife and daughters) the embodiment of English merriment and Christmas festivity. Unlike Scrooge, Fezziwig is ready to cast aside all signs of work to make room for Christmas festivity.

Little Fan is Scrooge's sweet-natured sister, who comforts him when they both are children. She grows up, marries, and dies young, leaving Fred, Scrooge's nephew.

Belle is Scrooge's fiancée, who breaks off the engagement because Scrooge has become unrecognizable to her by chosing to put more value on money than on love. Belle makes another important appearance later in her life, when, as a woman happily married with a lively family, she is a reminder to Scrooge of the abundant life he has missed out on.

The Ghost of Christmas Present guides Scrooge to several scenes of Christmas merrymaking. When Scrooge challenges the spirit about certain church policies, the ghost rebukes him with a reminder that the Christian verities that are supposed to govern the celebration of Christmas are often misunderstood and rerouted by ignorant and self-serving people to a different purpose. This ghost vigorously interacts with Scrooge. Like the first ghost, it is intent on compelling him to rethink his hardhearted positions. In the presence of Tiny Tim, for example, the specter reminds Scrooge of his callous disregard of the poor and disabled, referring to them dismissively as the "undeserving surplus."

The Cratchit family is emblematic of human warmth and nurturing—the family that Ebenezer Scrooge did not have. Anticipating the death of Tiny Tim, the family members pledge to balance their grief with the inspiration they have been given by the child's spirit of grace and gratitude.

Tiny Tim is the young, physically impaired son in the Cratchit family. It is impossible to lay eyes on him without being jolted into an awareness of the apparent injustice in the world: Why should the innocent suffer? And why, by contrast, should the miserly prosper? It is an ancient question, and Dickens does not have an answer, but with Tiny Tim (surrounded by his nurturing family), the author is able to dramatize the human capacity for selfless love. Most powerfully, Tiny Tim is an unnamed member of the population Scrooge dismisses as "surplus," the undeserving masses who cannot support themselves and therefore would be better off dead. Dickens uses the figure of Tiny Tim to give face and name to this group of dismissed and disparaged individuals.

Ignorance and **Want** are personified by two desperately poor and feral-appearing children, inspired by Dickens's visits to the so-called ragged schools in London, which were trying to get lost children off the streets and educate them. Dickens believed poverty and ignorance to be destructive and oppressive forces acting on these children who, without public intervention, would become dangerous to society.

The Ghost of Christmas Yet to Come is more phantomlike than the other two spirits, more ephemeral and inaccessible. Perhaps—given its already ephemeral nature—this ghost is missing the experience that would lend it substance and gravity. Perhaps as well its function is less to lead than to gently indicate the direction Scrooge already knows he must follow. The ghost makes its will known cryptically, using a pointed finger extended from an unearthly hand to indicate a general direction for Scrooge.

Summary and Analysis

Stave I: Marley's Ghost

The narrator of this ghost story does not inspire confidence at the outset; the more he insists on the certainty of Marley's death, the more uneasy readers may become about where they are being led and by whom. Even the sentence structure is disconcerting. What, for example, is beginning? This hesitancy, however, is the right tone; it focuses the reader's attention on mystery itself, what is seen and unseen, what is knowable or unknowable. With certainty suspended, we are made vulnerable to what may be coming. It is the right attitude for a ghost story. The narrator also sounds a bit daft; why speculate about how dead a doornail may be? Perhaps such concerns are included to encourage the reader to wonder about the nature of death, or perhaps it is a comment meant as humor intended to reassure us of the narrator's ordinariness—to get us to move back from the edge of our chairs.

Dickens invented Scrooge, but the character has taken on a life of its own since he first appeared. Paul Davis, who wrote a book about all the various incarnations of Scrooge, points out that the figure of Scrooge is as deeply embedded in our cultural imaginations as George Washington or Moses (Davis, 5). There is even a Disney version, Scrooge McDuck, the miserly uncle of three comical nephews. Scrooge's miserliness creates his miserable spirit, although he is unaware of this connection. Scrooge is also cold, detached, icy, with warmth equivalent to the single piece of coal he permits his clerk or the single candle in a cold room, barely able to sustain any life.

Scrooge is also a "loner," solitary "as an oyster." Self-isolating and miserable, he even scares away the dogs in the street and makes miserable nearly everyone around him—like his poor clerk, who must hover over the begrudgingly offered piece of coal to keep his fingers working to keep track of his boss's accounts. Into this bleak scene arrives Scrooge's incorrigibly unmiserable nephew, Fred, and the story begins.

It is the late afternoon of Christmas Eve and, except for the interior of Scrooge's counting house, a bustling and festive purposefulness prevails on the London streets. It was part of Dickens's intention (for the anticipated success of the story) to place the scenes pictured in these opening pages in an unmistakably urban setting. Depictions of Christmas celebrations commonplace before *Carol* first appeared were associated with rural life. Dickens's juxtaposition of bustling Christmas activity in the brown, foggy air and along the hard stones of the city's paved streets and sidewalks was deliberately established to inspire the English people dwelling in urban areas to participate in Christmas celebrations as fully as they had formerly done in their rural past.

Uncle Scrooge and his nephew have sharply contrasting personalities. From the outside, Fred brings his ruddy glow and steaming breath into his uncle's cold interior, but he is unable to spread any cheer. Interestingly, although Fred has neither guile nor ill will, he seems to enjoy how effortlessly he can outsmart his uncle's logic in an exchange about human happiness. Scrooge cannot understand how a person without wealth could be happy, but he has no answer—other than his famous "Bah! Humbug!"—to Fred's suggestion that, by the same logic, his uncle's wealth should be making him merry.

Dickens provides an early clue to the source of Fred's cheer: Fred has had a glimpse of life's larger purposes—a vision of the interconnectedness of the human family that is often obscured by the daily preoccupations of getting and spending but is reestablished each year by the return of Christmas. Fred explains to his uncle:

> . . . I have always thought of Christmas time . . . as a good time; a kind, forgiving, charitable, pleasant time; the only time I know of, in the long calendar of the year, when men and women seem by one consent to open their shut-up hearts freely, and to think of people below them as if they really were fellow passengers to the grave, and not another race of creatures bound on other journeys.

This powerful speech acknowledges mortality as the central fact of life, meant to govern all human effort and meaning. Its dominant place in the life of every mortal being creates a bond among people that dwarfs in importance any differences—political, ethnic, or cultural—that might appear to divide them. Dickens's choice of words—"people below them"—may sound unfortunate to contemporary ears but would have been fully appropriate for the highly class-conscious nation that nineteenth-century England was. Even then, Dickens's characterization of death would have been found by many to be appropriate no matter how a society organizes itself. We also know that this passage was important to Dickens; in his first public reading of *A Christmas Carol,* he changed "fellow passengers" to "fellow travelers"—a change that is important to understanding Dickens, because it introduces the notion that free will has a role in choices about our ways of relating to one another. Malcolm Andrews, writing in *Charles Dickens and His Performing Selves*, points out:

> It is an interesting change: 'passengers' denotes the passive occupants of a vehicle wholly controlled by its driver, whereas 'fellow-travellers' suggests a shared exploration of journeying. (24)

This notion of taking responsibility for one's direction and purpose in life—and of having free will to take that responsibility—is the foundation for the transformation Scrooge undergoes from being one kind of person to being a different kind of person. In this light, it is useful to note that, while Scrooge's spiritual conversion will appear to be a process forced upon him, in subtle ways, Dickens makes him a partner in the process, actually helping to bring it on.

At the beginning of the story, Scrooge is far from being capable of understanding the perspective described in Fred's words; in fact, his references to good cheer and his appeals to generosity elicit a stream of what might now be heard as alarmingly dangerous speech. One could even suspect Scrooge of being deranged. He is willing to inflict on any poor soul who merely utters the words "Merry Christmas" an especially gruesome punishment, reminiscent of medieval methods of torture. Such extreme language may communicate to readers that Dickens's story is creating an allegory with a timely message for his countrymen and -women.

Similarly, Dickens prepares his readers for the workings of the supernatural by introducing the ghost of Hamlet's father. The narrator needs a way to underscore not only the fact of Marley's physical death but also to put his readers into a respectful, even awestruck, state of mind to receive the full import of the story. Dickens—aligning his narrator with Shakespeare and invoking one of the playwright's most determined and credible ghosts, one that prompts Hamlet's questioning and leads ultimately to his conversion from grieving son to enraged nephew—achieves this effect.

Fred departs with all his Christmas cheer but is disappointed to have to leave Uncle Scrooge in his state of defiant and intractable ill will. Fred's departure ushers in two other visitors. The "portly" gentlemen are the philanthropists who make their annual appeal to those with wealth, asking for contributions to ease the plight of those in need. There is nothing especially offensive about them, but Dickens had short patience with righteous "do-gooders," perhaps because their strategies actually perpetuated the impoverished state of the poor rather than providing measures of reform that would make for a more equitable distribution of wealth.

Behind the exchanges between Scrooge and the charity solicitors are issues of social reform that were very much a part of public discussion in England at this time. Scrooge exposes the way he is imprisoned by the callous ideology of Thomas Malthus, an English economic theorist who argued in *An Essay on the Principle of Population* (1798) that exponentially expanding population numbers would outstrip a nation's agricultural capacity. Food shortages would create a "surplus population"—the poor—who would starve and thus be eliminated in the Darwinian struggle for survival. These arguments may have motivated Scrooge to question his nephew about getting married and adding to the population before he was earning enough to feed all his offspring.

Without apology, Scrooge believes himself, the hardworking businessman, to be superior to the poor, who are idle and therefore undeserving of charity, deserving only of their wretched fate. And with these Christmas Eve sentiments, Scrooge righteously dismisses the gentlemen and returns to work. A brief begrudging exchange with his clerk concludes the day and Scrooge heads to his melancholy tavern to take his meal alone. By contrast, Dickens gives us a happy glimpse of the clerk as he leaves his work: Poor as he is and inadequately dressed for the cold, he is nonetheless taken up by the excitement of Christmas Eve and joins in on some communal street play before going home to his family. While Scrooge is avoiding company, his nephew, clerk, and visitors are seeking out the company of others.

Dickens takes care to describe Scrooge's lodgings in such a way as to imagine the building as a once-playful child, "playing at hide-and-seek with other houses [who has] forgotten [its] way out. . . ." A drearier dwelling would be hard to imagine. The description effectively allows the reader to imagine Scrooge as he approaches the hidden and menacing entryway to his house. One way to make sense of the events that follow—beginning with Scrooge's seeing Marley's face on the doorknob—is to credit Dickens with foresight about psychological processes. When Dickens was writing *Carol*, Freud had not yet been born, but there were schools of study in hypnotism and mesmerism that anticipated Freud's theories and that Dickens was familiar with. It becomes possible in this light to think of Scrooge as a sick man who must enter a different world to activate a process of self-healing.

It is precisely at the entryway to his darkened dwelling that Scrooge's attention is caught by something out of the ordinary emanating from a familiar and ordinary object. In another flash, Marley's face appears on the door knocker, almost as if the "dead" man had residence there and was inviting his old friend in for a talk. The narrator has earlier insisted that Marley was "as dead as a doornail," so his living likeness appearing on a doorknob has to be a small and dark instance of Dickensian humor. For a ghost face, Marley's is not especially frightening, but it conveys horror nonetheless and startles Scrooge. Scrooge has his defenses, however. He has thoroughly divested himself of anything that could be thought irrational or supernatural. Being a businessman with no interest—as he informed his visitors just that afternoon—in anything not related to his business, he has shut himself off from all other realms of knowledge. He is, in effect, imprisoned in his world, as Marley had been. Now, faced with something unsettling that Scrooge does not understand, he goes inside. With the door closed and double-locked, Scrooge reverts to gestures and actions performed by scared children; almost comically we watch as he looks under the bed and under each separate piece of furniture in each room to be certain no menacing entity awaits him.

Readers familiar with the various routes available to those seeking psychological insight or self-healing will find none of Scrooge's thoughts or acts in this process mystifying. Several Dickens critics point to the parallel between Scrooge's encounter with Marley and journeys with the three spirits and the methods used in traditional psychoanalytic treatment. Joseph Gold, for example, points out that, even though seven years have passed since Marley's death, Scrooge has not troubled to replace the sign for the business; it still announces over the warehouse door: "Scrooge and Marley." Gold writes:

> If Marley and Scrooge are one, or parts of the same, then Marley's being dead would suggest that part of Scrooge is dead. Scrooge does not, of course, know that he is dead. He thinks that life in others, his nephew, for instance, is humbug, that is, pretense, cant, or delusion. Marley only discovered he had been dead in life after he was dead in death.

When Marley makes himself fully present to Scrooge, he appears in locks and chains, symbolizing his self-imprisonment. Scrooge has just come from three separate encounters—with his nephew, his clerk, and his visitors soliciting for the poor. Each visitor has made a similar request of Scrooge—that he, in effect, open himself up to others, unlock his heart and mind, and free his spirit so that it may encompass the realities of people other than he. Unconsciously, Scrooge may already have the sensation that his coldness and resistance to giving anything away are like links of chain binding him to a small space, namely, himself. Marley's appearance in chains is a jolting image, one that an unconscious mind might want to be rid of or to understand.

Two other physical features of Scrooge's residence prompt thoughts about other realities. The first is the illustration of Scriptures adorning his fireplace. These are mainly Old Testament stories about ancient people who have lost their way and are seeking righteousness and justice; or stories about conflict between brothers and nations; or stories that demonstrate the power of God's wrath in the face of human disobedience. By contrast, the teachings of Jesus, retold every Christmas, emphasize more of God's forgiveness and compassion. At the center of his teachings is the radical idea that the way people treat the most needy and sick among them is the way they express care for Jesus himself. Human beings everywhere are called on to act compassionately and generously with one another. The spiritual movement traced in both Old and New Testaments outlines the psychological trajectory Scrooge must travel if he is to save himself. The bells that suddenly ring out are reminiscent of church bells calling those seeking meaning and salvation to congregate and spread the message.

Consistent with other accounts of ghost visitation, Marley appears bearing physical traits and details—"pigtail, usual waistcoat"—sufficient to assure Scrooge that the visitor is his old partner. Even Marley's transparency—Scrooge notices he can see through Marley's abdomen—brings to mind the old rumor about Marley, that he was missing his intestines. Still not believing his eyes and determined to remain unconvinced, Scrooge tries to link his nightmare to some poorly digested bits of undercooked potato at dinner. Resolute, he "[fights] against his senses" until there is nothing left to do but address the ghost. "Who are you?" he asks.

Like most ghosts, Marley's appears to have a purpose and behaves reasonably; he even moves to sit down in a chair as if there were nothing odd about the scene. Still hoping bad digestion will be the explanation, Scrooge cracks an almost funny joke: "There's more of gravy than of grave about you, whatever you are!" Finally Scrooge is forced to come to terms with the supernatural event unfolding in his living room and ask his second question: " . . . why do spirits walk the earth, and why do they come to me?" With that question, Scrooge begins his spiritual journey; he will soon be dealing with mysteries far more complex than the formulas found in his accounting books.

The ghost of Marley comes with a single revelation and a single task. First, he announces that life continues after death for each individual, and the quality of that life is determined by the sum total of earthly purposes and preoccupations. He explains that he has been condemned to undertake his unearthly sojourn for seven years. His aimless wandering in heavy chains is his custom-made punishment for not having sojourned properly while alive, for not having made his way among his fellow mortals spreading "charity, mercy, forbearance, and benevolence." That mode of existence, he has learned in death, is the real "business" of life—not the professional pursuits he devoted himself to in life, with Scrooge as his partner, both narrowly focused on making and hoarding their money. This "business" the ghost speaks of is, of course, the personal pursuit Scrooge had just claimed to be the only worthy of his devotion.

Having imparted his revelation, Marley's ghost delivers the shocking purpose of his return. He has appeared before Scrooge to warn him that a similar fate awaits him unless he takes the second chance being offered by the ghost's visit to change his ways. This is an interesting proposition. Does Dickens intend to imply here what he seems to be implying, namely, that the universe must be governed by benevolent purpose if a single earthly life can be given a second chance to save its soul by changing its ways?

Marley's ghost announces the plan. Three spirits will visit Scrooge—according to their own timetable. Scrooge, anticipating the spiritual and psychological pain he is in for, makes a plea for delay . . . or, if not delay, for one visit from all three at the same time "to have it over [with]." Both Scrooge's hesitation and his eagerness to get this experience over with as fast as he can are feelings any mortal would recognize. Such responses are enough in this moment to elicit our sympathy. At the beginning of the story, we could not have anticipated this response.

No one knows for sure how familiar Dickens was with the writings of Dante Alighieri before the English novelist wrote *A Christmas Carol*, but a Dantean influence is clearly at work in the arresting panorama Scrooge faces outside his window after Marley's ghost slips out. One thinks of Dante's comment upon entering the circles of hell: "I had not thought death had undone so many." What Scrooge sees in the space outside his window are countless phantoms—ephemeral remnants of people once alive, now condemned by their choices on Earth to wander endlessly, moaning lamentations:

> Everyone of them wore chains like Marley's Ghost; some few (they might be guilty governments) were linked together; none were free.

Dickens's notion of guilty governments chained together by their cruel or unenlightened policies might be another instance of the author's dark humor. He provides an otherwise grim vision of the phantoms looking down on vignettes of earthly life—random and ordinary human situations where they could have given comfort but chose not to see or not to act.

> The misery with them all was, clearly, that they sought to interfere, for good, in human matters, and had lost the power forever.

The time for choosing to make the right gesture is over for these once-living, now dead and lost souls. The poet T.S. Eliot may have had both Dante and Dickens's Marley in mind when he composed his line for *The Waste Land* that describes the flow of Englishmen crossing the bridge on their way to work. Like Marley's ghost who remembers walking the streets at Christmas time with his eyes down to avoid contact with the merrymakers, Eliot's lost souls are oblivious to those around them.

Stave II: The First of the Three Spirits

For those interested in observing the close parallel between Scrooge's conversion experience and the psychoanalytic process, it is interesting to notice how he reacts to each step and the accompanying states of mind as he achieves his insights. Here, following the ghost's visit and being notified of the chance to change his life, he falls into a sleep so deep he thinks, upon awakening, that a whole day has passed. Scrooge has every resistance to learning anything about himself he does not already know, so it makes sense that he would want to fall into a long sleep as a form of escape. But sleep is also conducive to gaining insight; one thinks of the ancient tradition of looking to dreams for divine direction or a new perspective on an old problem. The couch in psychoanalytic treatment is used for a similar purpose. Sleep functions as a path to both denial and insight.

The first spirit arrives as promised at the striking of the bell. Again, as with the ghost of Marley, this spirit can be understood as a personification of some aspect of Scrooge, some earlier identity shaken off and forgotten, perhaps a tormented part of his personality. Its physical appearance—youthful and aged, adorned with both winter holly and summer flowers—suggests both the linear arc of life and the rhythm of seasons. Certainly the spirit appears to be a figure capable of wisdom and insight. Most astonishing about the spirit is the "bright clear jet of light" that springs from the crown of its head like a fountain of illumination, countering Scrooge's efforts at denial. Scrooge has a long and successful history of repressing thoughts about the supernatural, any kind of superstition, even the mystery of Christmas.

Once again, we see Dickens working ahead of his time; in this first stage of Scrooge's journey to insight, Dickens uses the potential healing power of memory. A person is always the sum total of his or her various identities moving through linear time, each personality appearing to cease existing as time passes but alive still in eternal time. Scrooge was once a child, once a youth, and a young man. Perhaps there is something deserving more than "Humbug!" that Scrooge could recover from this past. Leading him through that process is, appropriately, the Ghost of Christmas Past. "Long past?" asks Scrooge. "No. Your past" is the answer. At the mention of his personal past, Scrooge is seized by an impulse to put the spirit's cap on its head. What could be clearer? Scrooge wants to darken the light, to repress, as was his habit in life, anything personal or emotional, anything gotten through nonrational means. Scrooge, however, is in a new reality; the spirit is in charge and the light stays on.

Scrooge is soon overtaken by his first insight; "I am a mortal," he says, sensing he will fall when the ghost spirits him away. As Scrooge is led to the place of his childhood, he is engulfed with familiar sights, sounds, and scents. He responds with an unfamiliar emotion: excitement. "I was bred in this place. I was a boy here!" he says. When asked if he can remember his way, he exclaims with the exuberance that often accompanies memory. Dickens calls it "fervour": "Remember it! I could walk it blindfold!"

Details from Scrooge's early years stream before him, identified by the spirit as "shadows of the things that have been." Scrooge has been returned to a Christmas season from his youth. The general mood is jubilant until the sight of him abandoned in a schoolroom brings on a fit of crying. Critic Rosemary Bodenheimer points out why this scene is important: "Scrooge's ability to look upon his abandoned young self in the schoolroom brings self-pity; self-pity brings tears, awakening feeling; feeling awakens sympathy for others" (*Knowing Dickens* 66).

Scrooge next looks in on himself reading next to "feeble" fire in a rundown and melancholy house. He feels an air of "too much getting up by candle-light, and not too much to eat." Again, he seems to have been neglected, even abandoned. His friends from this period of childhood were imaginary—all characters in his books. The sight of this lonely boy brings forth in Scrooge his first experience of remorse. It brings to his mind another little boy, the one who just a day or so earlier had stopped before the office to sing a Christmas carol to those inside. Scrooge had ignored him; now he wishes he had given him something to thank him. His circle of awareness has now grown by one person. The carol the boy sings is the carol referred to in the work's title, "God bless you, merry gentlemen, May nothing you dismay."

We see for the first time—as Scrooge is seeing for both a first and second time—that his childhood was marked by many episodes of neglect, many instances when he was left to his own devices for comfort and diversion. The scene with his younger sister establishes the domestic disruption that seems to have always hovered in the background of his young life. Such sweet and pure devotion flows from sister to brother in this scene, but why would she be the member of the family sent to rescue him? What dire situation left him so neglected? Where was the now-welcoming father? We learn why Scrooge's sister is so important to him; she is the mother of Fred, his nephew, and her death at a young age brought pain to her brother's life.

Writing about Scrooge's change of heart, Dickens scholar Barbara Hardy observes:

> The return to childhood restores [Scrooge] to the first springs of love in a way reminiscent of Wordsworth and George Eliot; the personal past is a tradition which can keep alive the feeling child, father of the rational man. It also gives a brief glimpse at the deprived and isolated child. Instead of a recognition of causality—though I think that is obliquely present for the reader—we have in Scrooge himself the equally effective stirring of love and pity. He sees his sister . . . and the link is made with old affection and old sorrow. He 'feels pity for his former self' and the pity brings with it the first movement of imaginative self-criticism. (*The Moral Art of Dickens*, 35)

"The first movement of imaginative self-criticism": This is an essential component of the conversion process that Scrooge must undertake to avoid Marley's fate. Hardy's specific reference here is to the boy singing the carol.

The next scene from Scrooge's past takes place in the warehouse where he apprenticed. It is another Christmas season, and in this vignette young Scrooge is the subodinate and Fezziwig the boss. Scrooge's begrudging words to his clerk about getting time off at Christmas are contrasted with old Fezziwig's cheerful orders that work be set aside to make room for Christmas festivities. Young apprentice Scrooge and his co-worker exuberantly join the preparations and participate in the festivities. Old Fezziwig is jolly Englishness personified. His cheer and generosity draw together what sounds and looks like the entire population of the town. Everyone should have neighbors like the Fezziwigs: Mr. Fezziwig is so ebullient he "[laughs] all over himself," and a glow emanates from his body when he dances. Mrs. Fezziwig is "one vast substantial smile," and the three Miss Fezziwigs are "beaming and lovely." Under the influence of this joyful family, a workplace is transformed into a ballroom, labor into play, gainful work into communal celebration.

The chance to relive this scene in all its delightful and generous details makes Scrooge "[act] like a man out of his wits." The Ghost of Christmas Past, watching Scrooge as he is absorbing the significance of the scene, provides the words for what Scrooge must be thinking: "A small matter to make these silly folks so full of gratitude." After a brief calculation about how much of Fezziwig's earned income was used to host such a celebration, Scrooge makes a very un-Scroogelike speech: "It isn't [the money]. He [Fezziwig] has the power to render us happy or unhappy; to make our service light or burdensome; a pleasure or a toil. Say that his power lies in words and looks; in things so slight and insignificant that it is not possible to add and count 'em up: what then? The happiness he gives is quite as great as if it cost a fortune." Scrooge thinks of his own clerk and feels remorse for the second time, and his circle of caring expands to include one more person.

In the next scene, Scrooge's loss of innocence and preoccupation with wealth have begun to take hold. His one-time sweetheart tearfully breaks off their relationship. A young woman bidding farewell to her fiancé, she speaks with impressive composure about the choices Scrooge has made and why she cannot continue with him. He has replaced her with a "golden" idol and exchanged hopeful love for desire for wealth. She challenges him: Would he with his "changed nature," his "altered spirit" still choose her—a dowerless girl? Scrooge avoids a real response; her question is rhetorical. With her question, the young woman has bravely saved her own life; Scrooge's passive consent seals his fate. He will later feel this choice as deprivation. Scrooge begins his torment only after watching himself lose life's most desired gift.

One more painful episode of the past Christmas awaits Scrooge. It comes in a scene that could only have been written by one who—like Dickens—knew something about being the father of many children. It is another depiction of family warmth and comfort, but, in contrast to the Fezziwig party, the good feeling does not depend on wealth to make it possible. Instead, a happy marriage and a large, harmonious family account for the delightful scene of happy chaos that Scrooge sees. It turns out to be the modest home of his former love, who is enjoying the company of what Scrooge imagines to be at least forty children, romping around the living room and laughing. "The consequences [of all this playfulness] were uproarious beyond belief; but no one seemed to care; on the contrary, the mother and daughter laughed heartily, and enjoyed it very much."

Scrooge watches as the daughter plays with her future suitors and thinks of how he once was coupled with her mother. What Dickens gets exactly right here is the power of small details of recollected happiness to bring forth great feeling. If these are happy memories, they bring gratitude; but, if not happy, if one like Scrooge had deliberately walked away from these moments of life, they bring on remorse and a terrible sense of personal loss. Such it is with Scrooge, who says, in effect: What would I have not given to have been able to partake of this domestic joy. The playful joy comes to a halt as the father of the family walks in with a porter carrying a load of Christmas presents. An outbreak of "irrepressible affection" greets the father. This scene, followed by one in which the daughter sits with her parents by the fire, prompts Scrooge to wish for the first time that he had chosen a different life, one in which another daughter, "quite as graceful and full of promise, might have called him father, and been a spring-time in the haggard winter of his life. . . ."

During this first ghostly visitation, Scrooge must endure one more emotional assault: He overhears the husband describe to his wife a glimpse he recently caught of "an old friend of hers," Scrooge himself, in his dingy, cold office. In contrast to the warm interior of the family's home, it is a glimpse of human isolation and misery. It is too much for Scrooge; he begs to be rescued from the power of these moments, but the ghost reminds him that these vignettes are "shadows" of what Scrooge himself has brought into being: "That they are what they are, do not blame me!" Scrooge is tormented by the irreversible nature of each word spoken, each deed done in the earthly life. The scene ends in Scrooge's pathetic (but also almost comical) failure to extinguish the light used by the ghost to bring all these moments back into view. Like so many others who have been emotionally undone by events or feelings in their lives, Scrooge looks to sleep, which, as Shakespeare says in *Macbeth*, can "knit up the raveled sleeve of care."

Reflecting on the agelessness of the Ghost of Christmas Past, on its ability to change shape and move between different ages of a human life, Malcolm Andrews writes:

> This protean figure . . . is the agent of Scrooge's liberation from rigid introspective uniformity. . . . Itself constantly metamorphosing, the Ghost has come to disturb Scrooge into a recognition—first painful then joyous—of his true multifaceted self: surrogate father, uncle, child, businessman, pledged to live in the Past, the Present, and the Future. (*Charles Dickens and His Performing Selves*, 259)

Stave III: The Second of the Three Spirits

A warier and more prepared Scrooge awaits the arrival of the next spirit. Dickens writes: " . . . nothing between a baby and [a] rhinoceros would have astonished [Scrooge] very much." But Scrooge thinks he is ready for what is coming next, and then, as happens so often, the moment he thinks he has figured things out, something quite unexpected happens, which, in this moment for Scrooge, is nothing. Nothing happens, no spirit arrives; and this surprise sets him to trembling. He even imagines he might be about to undergo an act of "spontaneous combustion"—a fate Dickens liked to imagine and may actually have believed in.

Finally, in search of the next spirit, Scrooge walks into a room that is his own but utterly transformed—bedecked in all manner of Christmas decorations—winter greens and red berries. Scrooge also seems to have walked into a cornucopia of festive foods, an offering so massive as to be almost claustrophobic, as if all of London's restaurants, grocers, bakeries, butchers, and wineries had sent its foods and goods to Scrooge's household. A more informal, less formidable figure beckons him. It is the Ghost of Christmas Present, light filled and "glorious to see," a jolly giant of sorts, with many brothers. "More than eighteen hundred," it informs Scrooge (1,843, to be exact).

Actually ready—instead of resistant—to learn from the ghost, Scrooge lets himself be mysteriously transported to the streets of London on Christmas morning. It is a poor section of town with houses blackened with soot, dirty snow piled up under the newer snow, the air a "dingy mist," and the unpaved roads "thick with yellow mud and icy water." The streets are packed with people bustling in every direction. Despite the grimy surroundings, the people are out to have as much fun as possible. People shoveling snow off their roofs occasionally toss a snowball at each other, "laughing heartily if it went right and not less heartily if it went wrong." Even the food is animated—the fat shiny Spanish onions piled high in bins "wink" at the shoppers, and the lemons and oranges seem to be "urgently . . . beseeching to be carried home in paper bags and eaten after dinner."

Up to this point in the story, the polarities established—miserliness and generosity, poverty and wealth, the upper and lower classes—are familiar concepts. Most readers in Dickens's time were aware of these issues as well, and Dickens himself, as previously discussed, was not only devoted as a writer to dramatizing the plight of the poor, but at different times during his lifetime he considered taking other kinds of more overt action. The idea for *A Christmas Carol* came to him when he was especially caught up with these issues. The message of *Carol* associates Christmas explicitly and powerfully with a spirit of benevolence that would be necessary to inspire new legislation. Many Dickens scholars believe that Dickens's purpose in writing his story was ideological. He wanted everyone to internalize this spirit of benevolence, this Christmas message, and to use its power against the seemingly intractable problem (for the Victorians, no less so for our own time) of the split between the haves and have nots.

It would not be inconsistent with Dickens's purposes to question the efficacy of the Christmas spirit in addressing these issues or ameliorating the terrible conditions of poverty Dickens was portraying for his readers. Moral exhortations directed toward the middle classes to be materially generous to the working classes certainly relieved real suffering, but once Christmas passed and the goodwill incentives waned, the same conditions returned to keep the economic disparities intact. Implied in the messages to the middle classes was a measure of congratulation for being in the middle class in the first place. Some of the details of this dilemma come into focus in the scene in which Scrooge and the ghost are watching the people on the crowded streets of London going urgently to and fro, caught between the need to get their dinners (in this case their Christmas dinners) prepared for them by the bakers—a right granted the poor one day a week—and the obligation to heed the summons of the bells on Christmas Day and get themselves to church.

The English law that prompts the confusion in the streets was known as Sabbatarianism, a religious movement that sought to limit or prevent both commercial and leisure activities on Sundays and religious holidays. Its purpose was to ensure that the working classes went to their places of worship. Scrooge's moral conscience has been awakened just enough so far that he notices and is sensitive to the chaos imposed on the poor by having the sound of the bells' summons overlap with the time the bakers kept their doors open for the poor. He challenges the spirit to explain why in its name these religious laws are allowed to keep the poor from their meals and their leisure. The ghost has a satisfying answer—one that is familiar and still necessary a century and a half later:

> There are some upon this earth of yours who lay claim to know us, and who do their deeds of passion, pride, ill-will, hatred, envy, bigotry, and selfishness in our name, who

are as strangers to us and all our kith and kin, as if they had never lived. Remember that, and charge their doings on themselves, not us.

The next stop is the home of Bob Cratchit and family, and the scene is the family's Christmas dinner. It is a scene of domestic exuberance, verging on chaos. Feelings of goodwill prevail, and there is food enough for all. The long anticipated highlight of the feast is Mrs. Cratchit's famous pudding, described as looking like a "speckled cannon-ball, so hard and firm, blazing in half of half-a-quartern of ignited brandy, and bedight with Christmas holly stuck in the top." One can easily recognize in the appealing figure of Mrs. Cratchit the universal mother who cannot bring a prized pie or pudding to the table without apologizing for some imagined failing on her part sure to cause some imagined inadequacy in the flavor, texture, size, or appearance of her creation. The entire family is appealing; everyone pitches in to help, everyone is grateful for what they have and asks for no more when the dinner is over. They also enjoy one another's presence, recalling the family witnessed earlier that Scrooge might have had had he married his sweetheart.

As the family gathers around the hearth and the chestnuts are roasting (in a postcard vision of the family at Christmas), Scrooge watches Bob Cratchit with his son, Tiny Tim, and is struck, uncharacteristically for him, with compassion for the family and concern for the little boy's chances for survival. Before his eyes, Scrooge watches as his clerk, a mere functionary in the office, is transformed into a person in his own right, a father with a physically challenged son, a man deserving of respect and concern. Scrooge has also overheard Tiny Tim recalling the church service he had attended with his father earlier in the day. He said he hoped that all the people in the congregation who had noticed him could be reminded that the man called Jesus whose birthday they were in church to celebrate was the one who healed the sick and cured the lame. There is no self-pity in Tiny Tim's remarks—just a matter-of-fact willingness to allow his affliction to serve a larger purpose. Perhaps this quality of selflessness catches

Scrooge's attention; his own deeds have been motivated by a very different instinct. Perhaps, too, Scrooge sees that a person can possess more than one kind of wealth. Tiny Tim and his family are rich in spirit and in love—a concept that for Scrooge has been unimaginable.

Scrooge asks about the fate of Tiny Tim. The spirit claims to have no powers of clairvoyance, but it warns that only some unseen intervention can prevent what appears inevitable for Tiny Tim. Spirits, apparently, are capable of irony, for, once again, this spirit does not hesitate to throw back at Scrooge his own words uttered earlier about the sick and the destitute: "If he be like to die, he had better do it, and decrease the surplus population." Scrooge's journey has had some effect; he hears these words differently now that he has seen one to whom these heartless sentiments could be applied.

Just before leaving the Cratchit household, Scrooge overhears Bob Cratchit offer a friendly toast to his employer; it is a forgiving and generous gesture, indeed, and one not happily joined in on by Mrs. Cratchit, who refers to Scrooge, not unreasonably, as "odious, stingy, hard, [and] unfeeling."

Out on the bustling London streets again, Scrooge and the spirit encounter so many people heading to one another's homes that Dickens is moved to make another amusing observation: " . . . if you had judged from the numbers of people on their way to friendly gatherings, you might have thought that no one was at home to give them welcome when they got there." He could just have said: "The streets were crowded."

Scrooge has one last visit on this part of his journey—this time to the humble household of his nephew, Fred. As if to underscore a different perspective about where real wealth resides in the world, Scrooge is led over bleak and forbidding grounds to a section of the city that feels almost like a ghetto, hidden from view. Anyone traveling through this section past the ramshackle facades of people's dwellings would not fail to notice the strength of the people inside. Despite living in poor circumstances, the inhabitants found there are not just surviving; they are dressed up in their cheerful holiday attire, as ready as anyone to celebrate with good spirit. Even the men out at sea on Christmas Day are happy to be thinking Christmas thoughts.

Scrooge and the spirit arrive at the gleaming rooms of nephew Fred's house, identifiable by Fred's hearty and inimitable laugh. Dickens notes that laughter, like disease, is contagious, but laughter, unlike disease, contributes to health. Health, it is implied, is another kind of wealth; in this house there is plenty of laughter. Fred, too merry for his uncle, who earlier in the day had muttered his famous "Bah! Humbug!" at him for trying to spread some Christmas cheer, is now regaling his family about that very episode. Wise Fred does not condemn his uncle, noting that Scrooge's unpleasantness is its own punishment. More talk goes on about what Scrooge is missing out on—shared meals, singing, and pleasant games. This is, after all, the party he had been invited to and rudely turned down. At one point Scrooge appears almost to levitate, so moved by the sight of all these happy people having fun and rejoicing together that he seems lifted right out of himself. For a few moments, he allows himself to enjoy his liberated mood, and he actually joins in on a guessing game being played even though no one can see him or hear his answers (which are all correct).

What good is all this activity doing for Scrooge? If the ghost has arranged for him to have these experiences, some good effect must be intended. At the beginning of the story, Scrooge lacked even a scrap of self-awareness, but now for the second time on his journey, he hears other people talking about him. This experience—certainly painful—can be helpful to someone faced with the necessity of making personal changes. Fred's words convey both criticism and hope; he refuses to give up on his uncle, and his uncle hears that message. At the very least, Scrooge is witnessing two things he could not have imagined earlier, namely, that generosity makes people happy and, specifically, being poor does not prevent people from being happy. As Teresa Love writes, " . . . in no other story does Dickens make it more obvious that he equates a morally awakened soul with complete happiness" (*Seven Deadly Sins*, 42). Scrooge is not yet a morally awakened soul, but the journey he is on has pointed him in that direction.

Although reluctant to leave the merrymaking, Scrooge obediently follows the ghost to the next experience. Every vignette of human activity that the ghost has Scrooge witness, experience, or pass through reveals the same truth: The spirit of Christmas is a blessing when people make room for it in their hearts. Finally it is the Twelfth Night of Christmas and the lifespan of the Ghost of Christmas Present is coming to an end. One last vision remains, one that shocks and terrifies Scrooge. It is the two children, the boy representing Ignorance, the girl representing Want—both "wretched, abject, frightful, hideous, miserable"—clinging desperately to the ghost's robes.

Dickens's depiction of Ignorance and Want issues from his long involvement with the various groups in England working for reform in the child labor laws and related social problems. In 1838, he visited a factory in Lancashire and emerged declaring, "I mean to strike the heaviest blow in my power for these unfortunate creatures" (*Letters* I, 483–84). For personal reasons as well, alleviating the deplorable conditions of child labor had always been a concern close to his heart. But Dickens had no personal heroes who had suffered child labor, and it is generally understood, as Rosemary Bodenheim writes, that "the child figures of Ignorance and Want [who appear in the *Carol*] are the nightmare fantasies who replaced child workers in Dickens's imagination" (*Knowing Dickens*, 63). Another critic, Hugh Cunningham, writes in his essay "Dickens as a Reformer,"

> [Dickens landed his] . . . blow on behalf of poor children at work in *A Christmas Carol*. Two children, Ignorance and Want, symbolize [the dark side of] Christmas Present (*Letters* 3:461). Both pose dangers, but Ignorance more than Want. Dickens seems to have been more concerned about the lack of education for children than about the work that they had to do. He returned again and again to the dangers of ignorance" (*Companion* 166).

The two waifs, whom no one would wish to claim, nonetheless belong, according to the ghost, to all of us: "They are Man's," it explains. They are our responsibility. Of their faces, Dickens writes: “Where angels might have sat enthroned, devils lurked, and glared out menacing.” This must stand as a warning to society that attention must be paid. Children neglected, abused, abandoned, uneducated, malnourished, and oppressed will become depraved, and all of society will be threatened.

Stave IV: The Last of the Spirits

Scrooge has no respite between visitations; the third ghost appears as the second is fading away. Unlike the other spirits, this ghost—the Ghost of Christmas Yet to Come—is not festive or beckoning. In its presence, Scrooge feels dread—perhaps a sign that he is ready to face the worst his journey will present and come out a changed person. One significant change has already occurred: Scrooge no longer resists these visitations; he has arrived on his own path and found his own momentum. He even appears to take charge of his own journey. He names the ghost and anticipates what is in store for him. Despite feeling a new level of terror, Scrooge has become a partner in his own healing.

Led by a spectral hand behind a dark shroud, Scrooge encounters a group of singularly unattractive businessmen congregating on a city street. They are discussing the death of an unnamed man, and one of them yawns as if the dead person were of no account, certainly not to them. Only one has the slightest inclination to attend the funeral, and another will consider attending only if he can get a free lunch out of it. Scrooge is led on to two other men; these he knows well, “having made a point always of standing well in their esteem: in a [strictly] business point of view.” Whoever has died gets no good word from them, either. Dickens has created a poignant moment here: Scrooge is having to spend a long time not knowing the dead man’s identity, but he continues to trust that the experience is being arranged for his own good. To add to his confusion, Scrooge sees no likeness of himself when he passes his usual spot.

As if descending deeper into Dante’s circle of sinners, Scrooge follows the ghost to a section of town “[reeking] with crime, with filth, and misery” and finally into a shop of sorts selling a random collection of “iron, old rags, bottles, bones, and greasy offal.” A dead body lies covered behind a curtain, attended by four people, two women and two men. The place is a morgue, but their attendance has no reverence; they are laughing with disrespect, tainted by the ugly spirit of revenge. It becomes clear from the conversation that reverence is not intended. These are not mourners but plunderers of the body, scavengers of the dead. Scrooge, feeling more terror than he can express, thinks he understands the import of what he is witnessing: This scene might be a foreshadowing of his own end. At this point in his spiritual journey, Scrooge has developed some compassionate impulses toward others in need. He is moved by his observation that no one has any feeling for the dead man and expresses a wish that someone somewhere could be found who could produce some emotion, *any* emotion about him. Scrooge's wish is granted. He is brought to view a scene where an older couple is contemplating how they will fare after a man to whom they are indebted has died. The only positive emotion in the scene is the relief felt by the couple that a more understanding lender will take over the debt.

Scrooge is not satisfied; he wishes to summon someone to the scene who might have felt some tenderness, might have a single good word to say about the deceased. Perhaps this wish functions in Scrooge as an unconscious gesture toward self-respect or even self-love. Such an instinct is an essential piece of self-healing. Scrooge is then transported to the Cratchit home, where he finds the family in mourning over Tiny Tim, who is near death. Each member suffers his or her own private grief, but their interactions reflect care and compassion for the others who are similarly grieving. This is a family that gives strength and hope to each of its members. Bob, the father, has just returned from the cemetery where the family will bury Tiny Tim on Sunday. Assembling the family, Bob leads them in a pledge to keep sacred all memories of Tiny Tim and to allow the pure love of their little son and brother to protect and preserve the mutual goodwill of the family. "Spirit of Tiny Tim," says the narrator, "thy childish essence was from God." This scene is surely one in which someone is saying a good word—and much more—about one who is expected to die imminently, but neither Scrooge nor the unidentified dead man has any place in it.

At the site of the morgue, Dickens chooses to remind the reader of one of the messages in Fred's reflection on the meaning of Christmas. Death makes all of us "fellow passengers to the grave"; our deeds in life make for our immortality after death and represent the divine triumph over death. Dickens addresses death:

> Oh . . . dreadful Death, set up thine altar here, and dress it with such terrors as thou hast at thy command: for this is thy dominion! But of the loved, revered, honoured head, thou canst not turn one hair to thy dread purposes. . . . It is not that the hand is heavy . . . ; it is not that the heart and pulse are still; but that the hand WAS open, generous, and true; the heart brave, warm, and tender; . . . Strike, Shadow, strike! And see his good deeds springing from the wound, to sow the world with life immortal.

With that bold assurance, the fallen soul of Ebenezer Scrooge has arrived at the moment when he must look into the core of his identity and face the worst. It is he whose death no one mourned, his body that the ill wishers were plundering, his departure from life that caused indifference and rejoicing, not sorrow or gratitude. Scrooge's journey began in a state of righteous self-centeredness and ignorance and came to a bleak and ignominious end. Yet on the way he has acquired a measure of self-awareness and compassion. As it happens in dreams, both joyful and nightmarish, he awakens—alive and in his own bed; he watches as the disturbing presence disappears into a bedpost.

Interestingly, at the end of this stave or section, Scrooge is not intent on freeing himself from the ghost's presence; rather he is eager to say what he has learned about what he must do to turn his life to a different purpose. The ghost has run out of things to say. Scrooge is the one who feels compelled to speak. He pledges:

> I will honour Christmas in my heart, and try to keep it all the year. I will live in the Past, the Present, and the

Future. The Spirits of all Three shall strive within me. I will not shut out the lessons that they teach.

Stave V: The End of It

Scrooge awakens, beside himself with his new happiness and giddy with relief that he has been granted a second chance. He repeats his pledge to live in the past, present, and future simultaneously, although it is not clear what he thinks that would entail, or how, being human and living in linear time, he might actually perform this feat. Having lived for years in such a diminished and miserly state of mind, he has no room for the abundance of emotions he feels bursting within him. He laughs, cries, and jumps around—all at the same time—until he runs out of breath and has to stop.

Throwing open the windows onto a perfect winter day, Scrooge learns it is Christmas Day; he had not slept through it after all. His experience of the ghostly visitations—like the experience of time in dreams—occurred in a timeless state that can seem magically upon awakening to have spanned a year or a century but, measured in linear time, took up only a few minutes of the dreamer's deep sleep. Scrooge hails a boy on the street whom he sends to fetch a "prize turkey twice the size of Tiny Tim" to be sent to the Cratchit family.

Out on the streets of London, Scrooge is making up for lost time. He joins the flow of people and behaves like a man would if given a single day to follow every impulse, greet every person, think every thought that would customarily take a whole year to accomplish. Then he shows up at his nephew's home, startling everyone by announcing that he has come for dinner after all. The next day he races to beat Cratchit to the office, and when the clerk arrives, Scrooge feigns anger about him being eighteen and a half minutes late. Cratchit was expecting as much, knowing nothing of his employer's overnight conversion. Scrooge has good intentions this morning—he has decided to raise his clerk's salary and to follow up with other generous acts—but he lacks some skill in expressing them. Cratchit's customary reaction to Scrooge is apologetic and fearful, but when Scrooge leaps off his stool and gives him a good poke in the ribs, he becomes alarmed and fears the old miser has succumbed to lunacy. It turns out not to be lunacy; again, Scrooge's newly released energies, like his newly acquired social impulses, make for some strange previously unwitnessed behaviors.

In the final two paragraphs, the narrator reports that Scrooge was faithful to his pledge to renounce his old ways and live generously with goodwill for all. Tiny Tim does not die. He lives to bestow his famous blessing on the story and all its readers. The Christmas spirit has been triumphant.

What does a twenty-first century reader make of this story? The ordeal of conversion is a real process, a serious achievement, and not an everyday event. How does it happen? Dickens assures us that Scrooge's conversion was genuine and enduring, but he failed to convince Edmund Wilson, who writes:

> Shall we ask what Scrooge would actually be like if we followed him beyond the frame of the story? Unquestionably he would relapse when the merriment was over—if not while it was still going on—into moroseness, vindictiveness, suspicion. He would . . . reveal himself as the victim of a manic-depressive cycle, and a very uncomfortable person. (*Wound and Bow* 53)

But Dickens has given no more story to follow, and Wilson acknowledges in another section of the same essay that the figure of Scrooge is so embedded in our Christmas folklore that we forget to inquire into the mechanics of conversion. But the phenomenon of conversion was fundamental to Dickens; some form of it is present in most of his writing, and there is much about his use of it in Scrooge's life that is interesting to consider.

The dramatization of Scrooge's conversion has a magical quality about it that appears to avoid grappling with the psychological impediments and spiritual complexities of the process. Dickens readily acknowledged that he made use of the supernatural to expedite Scrooge's passage along the way. *A Christmas Carol* was intended to be read by his first readers as a parable with a fully accessible message. It would have been natural to understand the story allegorically; that is, it was about more than the personal transformation of a specific person. In the words of one of Dickens's best-known biographers, "[*A Christmas Carol*] is a plea for society itself to undergo a change of heart" (Edgar Johnson, *Charles Dickens*, vol. 1, 487).

So what did Dickens understand about conversion? Most profoundly, Dickens appears to have understood the importance of perspective in the process. In *Carol*, he writes, "In almshouse, hospital, and jail, in misery's every refuge, where vain man in his little brief authority had not made fast the door, and barred the Spirit out, he left his blessing, and taught Scrooge his precepts." The narrowness of human scope, the limited vision that comes from inhabiting a body fixed in a particular time and space makes it impossible to see the whole picture, impossible even to see from the perspective of another person, certainly not another ethnic group or a different nation. "Vain" because from such a limited space, it is easy for each individual to think he or she resides at the center of the universe, to think one's own perspective could possibly encompass all the truth in the world.

Scrooge, like everyone else, is afflicted with narrow vision. Some, as Dickens writes, have not "barred the Spirit out." The "blessing" left by the spirit is the possibility for wider perspective that enables people to live in a way that is more aligned with the larger truth of human interconnectedness. This truth, as Dickens wished to convey, is embodied in the spirit of Christmas. Dickens scholar Jane Vogel, who writes about the allegorical structure of his novels, observes about the vanity of "man in his little brief authority": "Such is the saving perspective on human life *sub specie aeternitatis* easily lost sight of in the hurry-scurry of life, and reacquired only in the celestial company of Three Spirits" (*Allegory*, 185).

How do we view the spirits? Do they represent interventions from the unconscious? Are they embodiments of ancient wisdom transmitted in different ways throughout the centuries? Looking at Scrooge, Marley's ghost asks, "Why did I walk through the crowds of fellow beings with my eyes turned down, and never raise them to that Blessed Star which led the Wise Men to a poor abode!"

We might ask why the transformed Scrooge did not make Cratchit his partner instead of simply giving him a raise. Such a question leads to a whole set of speculations about the Christmas message. As Joseph W. Childers writes, "Thus, Christmas attempts to curb the predatory aspects of capitalism, but never does away with it altogether" (125). But that was not Dickens's purpose. By creating the character of Ebenezer Scrooge as the literary embodiment of miserliness, Dickens dramatized the concepts of wealth and poverty in a way designed to move readers in a different direction. Scrooge's riches are another kind of poverty. Material poverty is still presented as the scourge it is, but the possession of wealth—represented by Scrooge and his partner—is no guarantee of happiness, nor does poverty, as he also dramatizes, make human happiness impossible.

The spirits enabled Scrooge's conversion by opening his self-absorbed mind to memory, specifically to memories of being loved and of loving. Barbara Hardy says, "Like all Dickens's Utilitarian egoists, [Scrooge] needs to have his heart taken by storm, and the storm comes in the shape of nostalgia, pity, and fear" (*Moral Art*, 34). And what does a Dickens conversion look like? It looks like a man weeping who has not wept for a very long time. It looks like a man falling into a swoon of remorse at the sight of life lost. It looks like a man who was ready to assign Tiny Tim to the category of "surplus population" who now plans to lend support to him and his family for the rest of their days. It also looks like a man jumping out of his skin because he can no longer contain the exhilaration of being alive. Critic Joseph Gold asks the question in a different way:

> Converted from what to what? *A Christmas Carol* gives the answer more precisely and more simply than anywhere else in Dickens—converted from closedness to openness, from frigidity to warmth, from isolation to brotherhood, from death to life. This is the meaning of Scrooge and Marley and this is the meaning of Christmas. (*Radical Moralist*, 148)

Critical Views

BARBARA HARDY ON THE INFLUENCE OF LOVE ON THE CONVERSION PROCESS

Moral conversion lies at the heart of many novels. And we might use William James's distinction between the sudden conversion, or *crisis*, of St Paul, and the gradual conversion, or *lysis*, of Bunyan or Tolstoy, to distinguish between *Robinson Crusoe* and *Martin Chuzzlewit*, novels of abrupt change, and *Emma*, *Daniel Deronda*, and *The Ambassadors*, chronicles of gradual progress. Although Dickens must be classed with Defoe, in structure and psychology, as a novelist of *crisis*, the moral implications of his novels place him with Jane Austen, George Eliot, and Henry James. Robinson Crusoe, on the Island of Despair, is converted by storm, sickness, and vision, to a faith in his guiding Providence, and his material rewards are considerable. Both Providence and material success are tainted concepts for Dickens, George Eliot, and Meredith, and the typical conversion of the great Victorian novel is not a religious conversion but a turning from self-regard to love and social responsibility. . . . The change of heart may provide the chief interest of the story, as in *A Christmas Carol*, a large part of the interest, as in *Great Expectations* and *Our Mutual Friend*, or a relatively unsubstantial part, as in *Martin Chuzzlewit*. It may play an apparently small part, as in Tattycoram's conversion in *Little Dorrit*, but illuminate much more than its immediate area of action. . . . All these examples of the change of heart have one thing in common: where George Eliot and James transcribe the moral process in slow motion and loving detail, allowing for its irregular pulse, its eddy, its wayward lapse and false start, Dickens shows it as quick, simple, and settled. . . . Love is relevant . . . to the discussion of Scrooge. Because this is the only example of an entirely fantastic treatment of conversion I should like to depart from chronology, and begin my illustration of this recurring convention with *A Christmas Carol*.

Marley's ghost wrings his chained hands as he contemplates the moral plight of Scrooge, and laments: 'Why did I walk through the crowds of fellow beings with my eyes turned down, and never raise them to that Blessed Star which led the Wise men to a poor abode!' (Stave I). Scrooge, like many another Victorian anti-hero, is the Utilitarian Wise Man, and he is forced to find the poor abode and forced to give. Before he can lift his eyes to the Star he has first to turn them on himself. Like all Dickens's Utilitarian egoists, he needs to have his heart taken by storm, and the storm comes in the shape of nostalgia, pity, and fear. . . .

Scrooge sees his own image in the most literal fashion, moving back in time and confronting himself at different stages in his process of deterioration. There is his old self, the child, loving and innocent opposite of the unloving old sophist. There is the transitional self, committed to loveless rationalism, but still holding some few warm contacts with the past. There is his mirror-image, the present self who echoes his own words and sentiments but in a context newly charged with feeling. The doubles, like the ghosts, are all potent in different ways, and indeed the ghosts are not only aspects of Christmas but in part at least aspects of Scrooge: his past, his present, and his suggestively anonymous future. The return to childhood restores him to the first springs of love in a way reminiscent of Wordsworth and George Eliot; the personal past is a tradition which can keep alive the feeling child, father of the rational man. It also gives a brief glimpse at the deprived and isolated child. Instead of a recognition of causality—though I think that is obliquely present for the reader—we have in Scrooge himself the equally effective stirring of love and pity. He sees his sister, rather as Silas Marner remembers his sister after he first sees Eppie, and the link is made with old affection and old sorrow. He 'feels pity for his former self' and the pity brings with it the first movement of imaginative self-criticism. He identifies his old sorrow with sorrow outside himself: 'There was a boy singing a Christmas Carol at my door last night. I should like to have given him something: that's all' (Stave II). This is of course the carol which gives the story its name, and also its theme: 'God bless you, merry gentlemen, May nothing you dismay.' Scrooge threatens the boy with his ruler, rejects the blessing, and Christmas brings him a strong but salutary dismay.

The Ghost of Christmas Past acts as devil's advocate, and his timing is admirable. Scrooge is identifying himself with his former self at Fezziwig's ball: 'His heart and soul were in the scene, and with his former self. He corroborated everything, remembered everything, enjoyed everything, and underwent the strangest agitation' (Stave II). The Ghost pours cold water on the apprentices' gratitude: 'A small matter . . . to make these silly folks so full of gratitude . . . He has spent but a few pounds of your mortal money: three or four perhaps.' So Scrooge is forced to defend the generous spirit, 'heated by the remark, and speaking unconsciously like his former, not his latter, self: "The happiness he gives, is quite as great as if it cost a fortune".' Then he suddenly remembers his present self, and gently urged by his ghostly analyst, moves towards self-criticism. The process is continued by the second Ghost, in Stave III, who answers Scrooge's anxious question about Tiny Tim: 'If he be like to die, he had better do it, and decrease the surplus population.' When Scrooge is overcome 'with penitence and grief' at his own words, the Ghost comes in quickly with the grave rebuke: 'forbear that wicked cant until you have discovered What the surplus is, and Where it is.' The Ghost employs the same mimicry when he shows the terrible children, Want and Ignorance. Scrooge's newborn horror, like his compassion, is answered by his own words: 'Are there no prisons? . . . Are there no workhouses?' This technique of exact quotation comes decorously enough in the Christmas present, rubbing Scrooge's nose in his very recent refusal to give to the portly gentleman. The arguments for charity were also presented in personification ('Want is keenly felt, and Abundance rejoices') but they have to be acted out for the unimaginative man, forcing him to walk through the crowds and see them composed not of ciphers but of individuals. All the elements in this brief masque are appropriate. They show the hardened man the need and love in his own past; they show the old killjoy his dead capacity for joy. Having indicated causality and change the show ends with a *memento mori*, cold, solitary, and repulsive, in the new perspective of feeling. Effective argument is implied in the dramatic reclamation by love and fear, and we are left with the urgent question—is reclamation still possible?—which makes the modulation from nightmare to reality. The fantasy has a realistic suggestion of hypnotic therapy.

JANE VOGEL DISCUSSES ALLEGORY IN *A CHRISTMAS CAROL*

At moments any Dickens reader will recognize that he has left the realms of realism behind and entered a *Pilgrim's Progress*-like world of giant symbols. As early as *The Pickwick Papers* many a 'Samuel Slumkey,' 'Count Smorltork,' and 'Bob Sawyer' thrusts symbolic interest blatant or subtle upon us: *Slumkey*, KEY to the SLUM; Smorltork, SMALL TALK. Bob Sawyer, whose sign reads 'Sawyer, late Nockemorf' (532), exhibits a Dickens both nimble and highly serious at such play. In medical student 'Sawyer' the 'Sawbones' (406), as Sam Weller irreverently calls him, 'Saw' proves a swipe at the breed whose indifference to life and limb of patients, to Sawyer & Co. mere machines for 'saw off' operations and fat fees, is tantamount to a policy of 'Nockemorf': *Knock 'Em Off*. . . .

Dickens constantly, and seemingly effortlessly, invents in this vein. . . . If Bunyan comes to mind as a likely model in symbolic portraiture of the kind (the 'Giant Despair' in *Chuzzlewit* and 'Giants Slay-good and Despair' in the essay 'Ignorance and Crime' two open Dickensian tributes to Bunyan), so might Shakespeare, Fielding, and others. The Dickens who, Forster relates, plays Justice Shallow in *The Merry Wives of Windsor* and Sir Epicure Mammon in Jonson's *The Alchemist* (FD, II, 364); who names a son Henry Fielding Dickens after the creator of that most symbolic-sounding personage, Squire Allworthy of Paradise Hall; who in *Copperfield* tips his hat to Smollett's Roderick Random, and in an

'In Memoriam' lauds Thackeray from whose pen symbolic worlds of 'Sharp,' 'Crawley,' and 'Sheepshanks' flow: this Dickens carries forward and extends a noble English comic tradition both 'Shallow' and Deep, 'Random' and Purposed, of 'Mammon' and God, half way and more to allegory: of easeful moralistic genius that instructs the better in avoiding too serious an air. . . . Come Christmas, and Dickensian allegory wears a holiday face wreathed in smiles like a holly-and-berry door knocker, a veritable Scrooge's nephew of a face aglow with brisk walking out of doors (man ever the *homo viator* of City pavements) and with the incurable hope of converting an avuncular world of 'Bah! Humbug!' to 'A merry Christmas, God save you!' Dickens, it seems, will settle for nothing less than the conversion of the Jews—and Christians too.

A Christmas Carol too imparts its holiest Christian message in allegory. Tiny Tim, we know, points to Christ; no secret here. As Bob Cratchit his father tells his wife: 'He told me, coming home, that he hoped the people saw him in the church because he was a cripple and it might be pleasant to them to remember upon Christmas Day who made lame beggars walk, and blind men see' (CB, 45). The child is a divine transparency: 'Spirit of Tiny Tim, thy childish essence was from God!' (69). It only remains, then, to recognize Tim as a spiritual sprite or sprig of Timothy, the youthful disciple of St. Paul, the frail and unwell follower whom Paul calls his child and son in Christ (1 *Tim.* 1:2). Thus seen into, Tiny Tim is like the shining star set atop the Christmas tree last of all amid a universal chorus of 'Ah!'

If Tiny Tim points to Christ, Jacob Marley and Ebenezer Scrooge point to Hebrew time and values past. Wandering in chains for eternity, Marley's wan ghost laments a selfish earthly life in which he never raised his eyes to (in his words) 'that blessed Star which led the Wise Men to a poor abode' (CB, 21). *Jacob*, Israel, rejected Christ and does so still. To see him, picturing what he was in life, or see Scrooge in his dismal room staring at fireplace tiles that depict motifs of ancient Judaeo-Christian history, scenes of Cain and Abel, Pharaoh's daughter, Belshazzar, and Aaron's rod, etc., is to grasp the deep-dyed Hebrew components of their souls. To be 'Christians' in such wise, Dickens shows, is in effect to be Jews. Indeed, *Ebenezer* is the name of the stone set by Samuel, Judge of Israel, to commemorate a Hebrew victory over foes. Ebenezer means: 'Hitherto hath the Lord helped us' (1 *Sam.* 7:12). Ebenezer is a stone, and stony-hearted Ebenezer Scrooge lives up to his name.

Thus in allegory the question is no longer only, Will Scrooge, coming to honor Christmas, save a crippled child, but: Will an Ebenezer turn in time FROM Ebenezer or B.C. spiritual ways of vindictive triumph over foes and misanthropic, embattled separatism (' . . . hath the Lord helped US') reminiscent of Israel's price in exclusive election and disdain for gentiles, TO the ways of Christ mirrored in 'Tiny Tim,' the child poor in spirit and of lowly origin, the 'Tiny' or fragile Christian enterprise debuting then as now and evermore in a cold world. In Scrooge's fanatical resistance to Christmas (Marley, who now sees all, resists no more) is symbolized Israel's blind refusal of its awaited Messiah, and entrenched, age-old enmity towards Christmas. It is all over with Scrooge's seven-years' dead partner, Marley (sad, ironic *seven*). But in this hopeful seventh anniversary time, will Scrooge finally turn from his and the Hebrew past and, in the spirit of sabbath and seven, looking up at last, see the Star?

Yes! Divine opportunity knocks thrice. Three Spirits guide Scrooge on a journey through time; one misguided earth-traveller is granted a privileged vision of the whole, *sub specie aeternitatis*. Changed wholly by what he sees, the worldling's 'wicked old screw' (6) Screw-Scroo-ge *thy neighbor* policy blown clean away (as if one could hold fast to the things of this world!), Scrooge awakens on Christmas morning—wakes as for the very first time, born again. The holy Ghosts are with him yet. 'The Spirits of all Three shall strive within me' (70), he vows. *Three-me*: he rhymes, suddenly all rhymes.

Wild with all happiness, frisky as a new-born colt (or soul), Scrooge scrambles madly out of bed this Christmas Day in the morning as from the grave of a long buried life, or waiting death, Marley's inconsolable ghost its symbol, of his soul. Rushing over, he flings wide the sash. The window open:

another coffin-casement sprung wide. Ah! Never before such 'golden sunlight; Heavenly sky; sweet fresh air; merry bells. Oh, glorious! Glorious!' (72). Ring out, wild bells! And Heaven and Nature sing. In such descent of radiance from above and rising up in exultation to behold it is previewed the hoped-for resurrection of man to Glory. Scrooge's irrepressible, endless capers, chortles, exclaimings may well recall a child's boundless delight in opening colorfully-wrapped gifts on Christmas morn, which, figuratively speaking, is just what is happening here. How surpassing good to be born again, *and*, of all happy coincidences, born a child 'at Christmas, when its mighty Founder was a child himself' (53).

Why *such* thanksgiving? Because, the long transfigured night of vision past, it dawns on Scrooge that golden sunlight below ('Oh, glorious!') prefigures ('Glorious!') Glory; that, hark, the whole caroling Creation—sun, air, sky, bells—like the lark at Heaven's gate sings. In Joe Gargery's words, What larks! This is surely no common joy, but tidings of comfort and joy born of revelation of the joy of joys, Jesu, joy of man's desiring. Of remembering Christ our Saviour was born on Christmas Day. The Eternal bursts in, finally revealed as the wondrous secret of all. The glory of the Lord *shall* be revealed! A 'Heavenly sky,' capital 'H' lofty, intentful, prefigures, promises—Heaven. In such dazzling sunrise, Sonrise; on earth as it is in Heaven. One gust of truly 'fresh air' blows a masking earthly usage from common sights, words, world. In short, Scrooge miraculously reborn intuits the world as allegory, a running figure of the life to come.

How clever the boy is whom he dispatches for the Cratchit turkey (a child ever the angel messenger in Dickens) Scrooge won't, can't, can not, *never can or will* get over. This is because suddenly the whole intelligent, intelligible, intellectually thrilling order the Creator built into Nature and world dawns upon his waking soul. Good Morrow! Dizzy and all but helpless with the wonder of it all, Scrooge grasps the simple secret of Christmas and the uncommon meaning of its dear, common sights. Once, Christmas for Scrooge was a time of feeling imposed upon, of a holiday for his clerk and alms for the poor extorted by foes. Now the reborn Scrooge knows it as a time when the soul of man in outpouring of gratitude inexpressible for the gift of a Saviour must give, and unrelieved of its burden of thanks, give still more. Never enough! In, as Dickens calls it elsewhere, 'the great forgiving Christmas time' (SL, 203), dare we imagine Scrooge dares hope himself forgiven.

The old, crabbed, sunderland 'B.C.' self is no more. The self that stood on the Law, dismissing two gentlemen come seeking Christmas donations for the poor with: 'Are there no prisons? And the Union workhouses?' (12); that in Hebrew fashion upheld the lawful charity, which in Dickens, is synonymous with service only in the letter, not the spirit of heavenly charity. Now, though, Scrooge realizes that Christmas marks the birth of a spirit of compassion and spiritual largeness not to be so confined. Coming to care tenderly for a crippled child, undertaking to relieve a humble family's sore poverty and to raise its hopes, Scrooge at last enters into full harmony with a Season in which, in Dickens's words, 'we celebrate the birth of that divine and blessed Teacher, who took the highest knowledge into the humblest places, and whose great system comprehended all mankind' (LLS, II, 400). Note, not a Chosen Few, but 'all mankind,' which sublime ideal shines no less bright in Tiny Tim's message to the world, one so familiar, it may be, we have ceased to see or grasp it any more: 'God bless Us, *Every One!*' (Italics mine).

In every nook and cranny of this magic time allegory gleams. Consider Scrooge's spectacular, prolonged fit of chuckling: 'The chuckle with which he said this, and the chuckle with which he paid for the Turkey, and the chuckle . . . and the chuckle . . . only to be exceeded by the chuckle . . . and chuckled till he cried' (73). Echoing still the joyous strain, never before such *ch*uckling, *C*ratchit-cherishing, and *c*abs to *C*amden town for the lad (Scrooge insists) upon a Christmas Day. In flurries of snowy 'c,' 'ch,' and 'C,' Christ particles loosed and scattering all over Creation, the boy is off like a shot after the gift intended for secret giving, the gift which, as in allegory itself, the giver remains invisible, the most selfless and so surely the best, truest Christmas gift of all. 'Chirrup,

Ebenezer!' (13), words which in Scrooge's youth signaled an end to business and the start of Christmas, the Season to be jolly, are heard again. 'Chirrup': *Cheer up*, merry gentlemen, let nothing you dismay! All is as it was. In one little child found in a poor abode, in Tiny Tims evermore, behold the emblem of the Christ child. 'O, come let us adore Him,' carols the *Carol*. . . . The yoke of Dickensian allegory is easy and its burden light. Tiny Tim, recall, hopes it is 'pleasant' for people in church to see him, a cripple, and so be led to remember Christ's kindness to the halt and blind. Note: in Dickens the living symbol more than the preached sermon strikes the Christian lesson warm to the heart.

Teresa R. Love Looks at Dickens and the Deadly Sin of Avarice

Avarice is one of the most demoralizing outgrowths of pride. The man who is given to self-conceit is led to seek that which enhances his importance. As the intensity of the passion increases, its victim becomes less and less concerned about any considerations which stand between him and his goal; once he has attained it, he becomes unconcerned about the uses to which his wealth might be put in alleviating the troubles of others and considers it only as a means of securing his own well-being. Thus, avarice is an absorbing passion which destroys a sense of obligation.[1] . . . The pride of the avaricious man leads him to seek security in a luxurious life, on the one hand, and to seek the respect of others through the position and power which he desires. Thus, characters such as the Podsnaps and the Merdles surround themselves with luxurious furnishings and enjoy the company of those who can help them get ahead financially and socially. Misers are also avaricious, and although they would seem to belie the theory that the avaricious seek luxury (since they usually live austerely), they still apparently believe that their wealth may secure good lives for themselves in the future and, possibly, for their heirs.

The number of Dickensian characters who may be classified as miserly is small when contrasted with the number of those who seek luxurious lives. One might consider as miserly the Smallweeds, Jonas Chuzzlewit and his father, and the early Scrooge. Barkis of *David Copperfield* is also pictured as being given to hoarding. Dickens disapproves of these because they are frequently ruthless in their methods of acquiring their ends and because they refuse to use their wealth for any good purpose. Misers feel impelled to excessive thrift: The Smallweeds are so intent upon holding everything they have that they indulge themselves only in the barest existence, and so does Scrooge. Dickens' main concern, however, is that the thrift of the miser does not stop with himself; in practicing this thrift on his dependents, the avaricious man jeopardizes the security of those who look to him for subsistence. Miss Smallweed considers the bread crumbs and the tea which she and her grandfather leave an adequate part of the wages for the services which Charlie renders, and Scrooge gives Bob Cratchit only fifteen shillings per week. As a result, these two are so underpaid that they cannot adequately support the families which are dependent upon them. But Dickens sees excessive desire for wealth as a sign of moral decay.

The tendency of the Christian religions to debase all things of this earth has caused many writers to refer to the wealth of this world as being of no more value than dust, when compared to that of the next. Thus, in his *Purgatory*, Dante gives a striking picture of the degradation of the miser by showing him as cleaving to dust.[3] The notion that the gold and silver of this earth are dust finds modified expression in Dickens. Since Dickens shows little concern about a traditional heaven, when he denounces the avaricious for their lack of charity, he does not do so with any thought of a supernatural calculator who balances each person's records and dispenses pleasure or pain accordingly. His system is no less hedonistic in its principles, however. The difference is that Dickens believes that the man who practices charity is storing up treasures for himself here on earth—treasures which grow as a result of the affection which kindness evokes, treasures which take the form of love, confidence, and gratitude. . . . What is it about an inordinate desire of wealth which kills the sense of duty? How specifically does such a desire affect the peace of the avaricious individual and of his society? A look at "A Christmas Carol" . . . may help to answer these questions. . . . It is in essence a story of the death and rebirth of a soul. Initially, we are given a picture of a man who is not only miserable himself but who makes everyone around him miserable also. His refusal to join in the spirit of Christmas is only an indication of the extent to which his soul has decayed, for Dickens believes that Christmas is the one time of the year when all men who have the least good-will within themselves are cheerful and charitable. Scrooge's refusal to contribute to a fund to buy food for the hungry is an indication that he is void of Christian love, which, in Dickens, is an essential ingredient in the concept of the spirit of Christmas. By using the machinery of the ghost, the novelist is able to show, through a series of flashbacks, the progression of Scrooge from a lovable and innocent child to the most miserable of men. As he grows up and becomes more engrossed in the ways of the world, his sweetness turns to gall. By the time he has become a successful businessman, Scrooge has become so changed that his fiancée no longer feels herself bound to the same man.

As the ghosts of Christmas Past and of Christmas Present appear, Scrooge's reclamation begins. He remembers little deeds of kindness that he might have done. As he remembers these, we become aware of the complete happiness which will be his once he has become thoroughly charitable. In fact, one may say that in no other story does Dickens make it more obvious that he equates a morally awakened soul with complete happiness.

Notes

1. *Encyclopedia of Religion and Ethics*, II, p. 261.
3. *Encyclopedia of Religion and Ethics*, II, p. 261.

Paul Davis on Scrooge's Numerous Selves and Dickens's Social Gospel

Theologically, *A Christmas Carol* is an early version of what came to be known later in the century as "the social gospel." Centering its doctrine on the belief that the kingdom of God would be realized on earth, the social gospel movement saw history as an evolution toward this emerging Christian society. The family, led by a dominant and loving father, was its model in small of the Christian kingdom. The experience of conversion revealed itself in commitment to this earthly kingdom and in the performance of good works.[48] This doctrine, particularly prevalent in the United States from about 1880 on, had its roots in Evangelical social concern, in the social theology of F. D. Maurice developed during the thirties and forties, and in Unitarianism, with which Dickens was involved in the mid-1840s. Dickens may have arrived at his social gospel from these influences that were at work at the time he was writing. Its presence in the *Carol* made his tale particularly apropos in the decades after his death when the social gospel movement was ascendant.

As "social gospel" *A Christmas Carol* is the story of the Cratchit family. In evolutionary terms they represent a stage in human development beyond Scrooge, for they have transcended the competitive ethic of laissez-faire capitalism to create a family/community based on love, self-sacrifice, and sympathy. The *Carol* is less explicit in presenting this evolutionary motif than *Dombey and Son*, published four years later, where the Tootle family, linked to the emerging world of the railroad, represent a similar advance in human relations. At the center of the Cratchit Christmas story is the family's love feast, their Christmas dinner emblematic of the Christian tradition of agape.[49] This scene centered later Victorian versions of the *Carol*. One popular abridgement reprinted only the account of the Cratchit dinner as presenting the essence of the story.[50]

The father of this model community, Bob Cratchit represents its values to his family when he encourages his children in Christian behavior and chides Mrs. Cratchit for refusing to toast Scrooge as "the Founder of the Feast" (*CB*, 48). When Peter puts on his father's "monstrous shirt collar (Bob's private property, conferred upon his son and heir in honor of the day)," he represents the priority this Christian community places on sharing and its rejection of the preeminence of private property (p. 44). He also becomes a smaller version of Bob, and the family's conversation about his imminent entry into the workplace calls up visions of him as the Cratchit man of the next generation, breadwinner and loving father to his own family.

Bob's importance as father places him and his family in sharp contrast to Scrooge. Scrooge's father is absent from his son's life. As a child Scrooge is abandoned by his father to lonely schoolrooms. As a young man, Scrooge seeks opportunity in the city and, like many other uprooted economic migrants of his generation, he is cut off from family and home. Guided by what Ruskin called "the gospel of getting on," Scrooge rejects family and withdraws into lonely bachelorhood. He is not a father himself and is essentially fatherless.

The social gospel in America emerged, in part, as a theology for a new generation in the industrial cities, a generation no longer preoccupied with running to the economic frontier for new opportunity. Its familial ideal, an image of human interdependence and sharing, replaced the earlier ideal of the economic individualist seeking fulfillment on his own. A settled urbanite, Cratchit represents the father of the new social gospel generation. As he guides his children to a life in the city similar to his own, his example enables the reformed and "fatherless" Scrooge to become a second father to Tim and adopt a role he has not known earlier in his life.[51]

In the late-Victorian Holy Family, the father takes precedence over the mother, for it is his vital presence in this miniature Christian community that marks its difference from the dislocated families of the early industrial period, when economic necessity often separated the father from his wife and children. In the late-Victorian *Carol* as displaced Christmas story, Bob and Tim replace the Madonna and child. The image of Bob holding Tiny Tim emerges as the central icon of the tale, a symbolic representation of the patriarchal Victorian ideal. . . . Perhaps the most crucial moment in Dickens' reading of the *Carol* came when Bob Cratchit mourned the death of Tiny Tim. The New York *Nation* noted that Dickens made "a 'point' of [this moment] more decidedly than of any other passage in the evening's entertainment."[53] Although Kate Field found it overdone, observing that "here, and only here, Dickens forgets the nature of Bob's voice, and employs all the powers of his own, carried away apparently by the situation," most of his audience were deeply moved by what Charles Kent described as "a long-suppressed but passionate outburst of grief."[54] The change in Dickens' voice may have been deliberate, but it was probably a case of the storyteller being drawn into the story and moved by it as if he were a participant. Clearly Dickens hoped that his voice would draw the audience into the story and move them as well, as Kent said it did, so that "Bob's tearful outcry brimmed to the eyes of those present a thousand visible echoes."[55] The conversion experience of the *Carol* could not be Scrooge's alone. Becoming like Bob a father to Tiny Tim, needed to be the collective experience of all who read or heard the message of this social gospel.

Barry Qualls characterizes Carlyle's idea of the conversion necessary for nineteenth-century man as the "defeating of solipsism by confronting the self's demons and madness and reaching outwards toward others."[56] Scrooge enacts this pattern as he is transformed from the "solitary oyster" seeking only his own self-interest into Tiny Tim's second father. In the process he restores fatherhood to the secular city where God has died and the father has disappeared. His good works will become the healing spring to transform the city into the kingdom of God on earth.

When Dickens brought his social gospel to Boston in 1867, the healing power of his message was felt by many, including Mr. Fairbanks, a manufacturer of scales from St. Johnsbury, Vermont. During the reading Fairbanks's wife noted that her husband's "face bore an expression of unusual seriousness." Afterwards he confided to her that he felt he "should break the custom we have hitherto observed of opening the works on Christmas Day."[57] Not only did he close his factory for Christmas from 1867 onward, but also every Christmas Eve he sent each factory hand home with a turkey for the holiday, becoming, like Scrooge, "the Founder of the Feast."

Notes

48. For a detailed account of the theology of the social gospel movement in the United States, see Janet Fishburn, *The Fatherhood of God and the Victorian Family: The Social Gospel in America* (Philadelphia: Fortress Press, 1981).

49. For a discussion of Dickens' use of the Christian love feast, see Thomas L. Watson, "The Ethics of Feasting: Dickens' Dramatic Use of Agapé," in Thomas A. Kirby, ed., *Essays in Honor of Esmond Linworth Marilla* (Baton Rouge: Louisiana State University Press, 1971), pp. 243–52.

50. A Victorian version that reduced the story to the Cratchit's Christmas was *Their Christmas Dinner* (New York: G. R. Lockwood, [1884]); later such versions include *The Cratchits' Christmas* (Waverley, Mass.: Millpond Press, 1912) and *Tiny Tim's Christmas Dinner* (Los Angeles: A. E. Bell, 1927).

51. Scrooge has, in fact, consciously rejected a paternal role. When his sister Fan died, he apparently had a chance to become a second father to her orphaned son, Fred, but turned his back on the opportunity.

53. Quoted in Collins, *Carol*, 201n.

54. Field, *Pen Photographs*, p. 35; Kent quoted in Collins, *Carol*, 201n.

55. Kent quoted in Collins, *Carol*, 201n.

56. Qualls, *Secular Pilgrims*, 27.

57. Gladys Storey, *Dickens and Daughter* (London: Frederick Muller, 1939), 120–21.

* * *

Dickens' first experiment with the "Christmas book," the *Carol* departed from the formula he used in his longer novels. In *Nicholas Nickleby*, *Martin Chuzzlewit*, and *David Copperfield*, he centered the novel on a young man coming of age who wondered, as David Copperfield does, whether he would "turn out to be the hero of [his] own life." With some variations, even *Oliver Twist* and *The Pickwick Papers* can be seen as versions of this quest for identity. The antagonist to the hero in these tales is often a greedy "uncle" or surrogate father, a figure like Ralph Nickleby or old Martin Chuzzlewit who frustrates the hero's quest. When the hero discovers his identity, defeats or transforms the interfering uncle, and establishes himself in the world, his quest is completed.

A Christmas Carol reverses the usual positions of protagonist and antagonist. The villain is given the central role and his negative presence obscures the quest story. Although attempts to place the Cratchits in the center of the *Carol* try to restore something closer to the usual Dickens plot, the figure who most resembles the Dickens hero is not Bob Cratchit but rather Fred, Scrooge's nephew. His suppressed story is that of a young man whose worldly advancement is frustrated by Scrooge's objections to his good humor, his marriage, his whole way of life. Scrooge's role in dashing his nephew's prospects is hinted at in Fred's wife's observation during the Christmas party that Scrooge must be very rich, and in Fred's reply that Scrooge's wealth is of "no use to him" because "he hasn't the satisfaction of thinking—ha, ha, ha!—that he is ever going to benefit US with it" (*CB*, 52). In *Nickleby* or *Chuzzlewit*, this economic conflict would motivate the plot. Some versions of the *Carol* try to bring this subtext to the surface by making Scrooge's interference in Fred's life more active. In these adaptations, Fred is often portrayed as engaged and putting off his wedding until he can afford to marry, while Scrooge becomes an active villain by denying Fred financial help and thus preventing the marriage. After his Christmas transformation in this plot of fortune, Scrooge, like old Martin Chuzzlewit, shares his money with his nephew, usually by taking him into partnership, and enables him to marry. These changes, as in the 1938 Hollywood film starring Reginald Owen, could make the *Carol* more conventionally acceptable to the popular audience, but they suppressed much of the complexity in the character of Scrooge.

Making the *Carol* the story of Cratchit also simplified its center. Some readers could take ideological consolation in the transfer of economic power to the workers, but in such tracts Scrooge was flattened into either a stereotypical capitalist or an incipient Owenite. And the Cratchits, as good as they are, for most modern readers are just not interesting. Despite attempts in the thirties and forties to enlarge the role of the clerk and his family, many readers would have agreed with T. P. McDonnell "that Cratchit was an insufferable bore, . . . a whimpering fool."[9] To admit this possibility and not reject the story altogether called for recentering the *Carol* in the problematic character of its villain-hero.

The central fact of Scrooge's life is his conversion, but he is remembered as the ogre of Stave 1 rather than the kindly grandfather of Stave 5. He has entered the language as a lowercase noun to describe the hardhearted miser. The attraction of the villainous Scrooge may derive from the human fascination with evil that makes Satan more interesting than God. It also arises from his complexity. Scrooge can be reduced to a type—a miser, a cruel uncle, an ogre—but his character contains energy and complexity that belie such simplification. The divisions within him make him more even than "two Scrooges."

Some of the many versions of Scrooge appear in the various Carols of the story's first century. The *Carol*'s first readers were likely to see Scrooge as a representative of moral tradition, an emblem of "the Miser" whose preoccupation with money kills his altruistic impulses. Scrooge also engaged the sympathy of his first readers with a biography linking his experience with that of many city dwellers in the first half of the nineteenth century. Displaced from country into town and cut off from family and tradition, this Scrooge embodied their sense of urban anomie. As later Victorians consecrated the *Carol* with semireligious authority, Scrooge became a pilgrim, a fourth wise man seeking the "poor man's child" who would restore (and "restory") Christmas and the Christian message. At the turn of the century in the *Carol* as children's story, readers repressed the evil in Scrooge to focus on the kindly grandfather of Stave 5. Depression idealism discovered the potentially benevolent businessman whose reformation would break the chains of economic necessity. There is something of Scrooge in all these versions of his character. Defined by complexity and contradiction that make him both villain and hero, Scrooge embodies a tension between judgment and sympathy. Exploring this contradiction, Dickens countered the harsh sentences that hanged Fagin, Bill Sikes, and Ralph Nickleby and redeemed his own fascination with evil.

Postwar readers recognized in Scrooge a soulmate to Hermann Hesse's *Steppenwolf*. In that novel Harry Haller, tormented by the contradiction between man and beast within him, retreats from the world, fearing that his personality has been irreconcilably split. When he enters a visionary "magic theater," similar to the dream-world of Scrooge's Christmas spirits, he learns that he is not simply two selves, but rather a multitude of complementary and contradictory persons. Scrooge transcends the "two Scrooges," Edmund Wilson's Jekyll–Hyde characterization of him at the end of the 1930s, in the magic theater of Anglo-American culture during the thirty years after World War II. There he is performed as economic man, as a Freudian case history, as a creature of myth, as a spiritual father to the youth revolution of the late sixties and early seventies. Could Scrooge have worried, like Harry Haller, about the division in his personality, he might have been consoled in this series of transformations with Haller's recognition that "man consists of a multitude of souls, of numerous selves."[10]

Notes

9. "Was Scrooge Right?" *Catholic World* 180 (December 1954): 183–84.

10. *Steppenwolf*, ed. Joseph Mileck (New York: Holt, Rinehart, Winston, 1963), 192.

Donald R. Burleson on the Portrayal of Uncle and Nephew

It would seem that there could be no clearer or more unambiguously delineated an opposition than that which occurs in Dickens's *A Christmas Carol* when Scrooge's nephew comes to invite his uncle to Christmas dinner. The nephew delivers his oft-quoted encomium of Christmas as "a good time: a kind, forgiving, charitable, pleasant time," and Scrooge makes his own distaste for the Yuletide season abundantly plain. The opposition is one universally familiar: the Christmas-loving nephew's outgoing good-heartedness versus Scrooge's Christmas-hating miserliness and meanness of spirit. However, this supposedly stable bipolarity is one that the text itself subtly deconstructs in such a way as not merely to make problematic the logic of the opposition, but to deepen, as well, the textual significance of the famous Christmas eve encounter.

Scrooge's visitation by his nephew creates the impression of being a sort of ritual dance, a double posturing wherein each partner is a complementation-figure to the other. The chorus-like, stichomythic exchanges—"Uncle!" and "Nephew!"—tend to heighten this impression. But it is precisely in this ritualistic exchange that the textual voices unwittingly exchange also something of their roles, as they discuss the question of time (a key concern, of course, throughout).

It is the obdurate and truculently unfestive Scrooge who describes Christmas as "a time for finding yourself a year older"—the nephew's year, reckoned from Yuletide to Yuletide—"and not an hour richer." Curiously, with this remark he adopts Christmas as his very paradigm for structuring and measuring time, for defining the beginning and the endpoint of an elapsed year in one's life; he thus centralizes that which he purports to dismiss.

On the other hand, the nephew's own express mode of measuring time resides in his reference to Christmas as "the only time I know of, in the long calendar of the year"—Scrooge's year, the year of ledgers and fiscal legalities—"when men and women seem by one consent to open their shut-up hearts freely. . . ." In the nephew's remark, the calendar year is a structural *donnée*, an established and standard temporal spectrum on which Christmas ("when it has come round") is a lone point preceded by and followed by other points. The nephew thus marginalizes what he purports to centralize, in a manner complementary to that in which Scrooge centralizes what he presumably means to marginalize.

The point is that the dichotomy of character is not so sharply drawn as one might suppose, in that the syntactic flirting of each party with notions supposedly characteristic only of the other party allegorically points up the covert presence, in each character, of an essential trace of the other. Textual evidence abounds. The nephew, after all, does mention Scrooge's wealth as a reason why one ought not to be "dismal" and "morose"; he is thus perhaps not so unmaterialistic as he pretends. Conversely, it is obvious that Scrooge could scarcely undergo so radical a metamorphosis as he later does without possessing some seed of redeemability. But it is the language of the two characters' encounter that first allegorizes their mutual complicity with each other's traits and suggests, early on, that the text cannot be taken to support any too simplistic or reductive a view of human nature.

R.D. Butterworth on the Work as a Blend of Novel and Masque

In his Preface to the First Cheap Edition of *A Christmas Carol*, Dickens wrote of his intention in writing his Christmas books of awakening some "loving and forbearing thoughts" by means of "a whimsical kind of masque" (xiv).[1] Commentators have not made much of this comment, perhaps on the assumption that Dickens's familiarity with masques could not but be slight. This, however, is an unwarranted assumption. Examination of the contents of Dickens's library, as listed in the inventory of his belongings made when the family went to Italy in 1844 (*Letters* 4: 711–25) reveals that it was at least possible for the writer to have been thoroughly acquainted with the masque form. . . . Though the possession of such books proves merely that Dickens had access to detailed information about the masque form, he had, furthermore, witnessed actual performances of at least some versions of masque. During his 1842 visit to America, for instance, a performance was mounted of a masque specially written in his honor, "Boz! A Masque Phrenological," the characters in which included Boz himself, some characters from his novels, and figures such as Identity, Mirth and Wonder (House 3: 19–20). He had also twice seen presentations of "Comus" in 1843,[3] even appending a brief critical comment about the first to a lengthy review for *The Examiner* of the production of "Much Ado About Nothing" that accompanied it.[4]

Dickens, then, certainly had some acquaintance with, and was in a position to know a great deal about the masque; and to examine *A Christmas Carol* is to see that Dickens is making no idle comment in linking the work to the masque tradition. It is necessary, for instance, to look no further than the description of the Spirit of Christmas Past in Scrooge's chambers to detect the relationship:

> It was his own room. There was no doubt about that. But it had undergone a surprising transformation. The walls and ceiling were so hung with living green, that it looked a perfect grove; from every part of which, bright gleaming berries glistened. The crisp leaves of holly, mistletoe, and ivy reflected back the light, as if so many little mirrors had been scattered there; and such a mighty blaze went roaring up the chimney, as that dull petrification of a hearth had never known in Scrooge's time, or Marley's, or for many and many a winter season gone. Heaped up on the floor, to form a kind of throne, were turkeys, geese, game, poultry, brawn, great joints of meat, sucking-pigs, long wreaths of sausages, mince-pies, plum puddings, barrels of oysters, red-hot chestnuts, cherry-cheeked apples, juicy oranges, luscious pears, immense twelfth-cakes, and seething bowls of punch, that made the chamber dim with their delicious steam. In easy state upon this couch, there sat a jolly Giant, glorious to see; who bore a glowing torch, in shape not unlike Plenty's horn, and held it up, high up, to shed its light on Scrooge, as he came peeping round the door.
>
> 'Come in!' exclaimed the Ghost. 'Come in! and know me better, man! . . . I am the Ghost of Christmas Present,' said the Spirit. 'Look upon me!'
>
> Scrooge reverently did so. It was clothed in one simple green robe, or mantle, bordered with white fur. This garment hung so loosely on the figure, that its capacious breast was bare, as if disdaining to be warded or concealed by any artifice. Its feet, observable beneath the ample folds of the garment, were also bare; and on its head it

> wore no other covering than a holly wreath, set here and there with shining icicles. Its dark brown curls were long and free; free as its genial face, its sparkling eye, its open hand, its cheery voice, its unconstrained demeanour, and its joyful air. Girded round its middle was an antique scabbard; but no sword was in it, and the ancient sheath was eaten up with rust. (39–40)

This is a scene with all the spectacle of masque: it has the characteristic elaboration of "set" and costume. The spirit, furthermore, is one of masque: the reader needs no prompting to look for symbolism in the scabbard with its sheath eaten up with rust or the Spirit's free-flowing hair than would the spectators of a masque. In the manner of masque, the scene draws for its symbolism on both the classical tradition (the "glowing torch in shape not unlike Plenty's horn") and on traditional imagery taken from nature ("the crisp leaves of holly, mistletoe, and ivy"; the greenness of the Spirit's robe and the holly wreath it wears). Every detail at once adds to the splendor of the scene in being ornamental and is symbolic. The action of the scene, such as it is, consists of symbolic movement (the Spirit lifting up the torch "to shed its light on Scrooge") and declamatory speeches. There is, furthermore, a heightened quality to the dialogue of the scene, including even Scrooge's dialogue. At the beginning of the book, Scrooge's speech is characterized by features reflecting both normal conversational patterns and his own individual speech habits: his dialogue is full of contractions, interjections, vigorous exclamations, the aggressive use of questions, and a general informality:

> 'Don't be cross, uncle!' said the nephew.
>
> 'What else can I be,' returned the uncle, 'when I live in such a world of fools as this? Merry Christmas! Out upon merry Christmas! What's Christmas time to you but a time for paying bills without money; a time for finding yourself a year older, but not an hour richer; a time for balancing your books and having every item in 'em through a round dozen of months presented

dead against you? If I could work my will,' said Scrooge indignantly, 'every idiot who goes about with "Merry Christmas" on his lips should be boiled with his own pudding, and buried with a stake of holly through his heart. He should!' (9–10)

At times during the visits of the Spirits, when he is excited, Scrooge falls back into such habits ("Why, it's old Fezziwig! Bless his heart; it's Fezziwig alive again!" [30]); but generally his speech is more formal, as in this scene:

'Spirit,' said Scrooge submissively, 'conduct me where you will. I went forth last night on compulsion, and I learnt a lesson which is working now. To-night, if you have aught to teach me, let me profit by it.' (40)

This is language of a high order for the man who crisply summed up Christmas as "Humbug!" (40).[5] . . . It is, perhaps, the episode of the visit of Marley's Ghost, which constitutes the induction to the masque, that most clearly demonstrates the nature of the hybrid of novel and masque that Dickens is creating. The visit takes place at a significant point, as the narrative begins to modulate from the everyday settings, characters and events of the novel toward those of the masque that are to occupy the central portion of the work. There have been transformations of the knocker into Marley's head and back again, unexplained noises, and the flying open of a cellar door. Finally the figure comes before Scrooge:

Marley in his pigtail, usual waistcoat, tights and boots; the tassels on the latter bristling, like his pigtail, and his coat-skirts, and the hair upon his head. The chain he drew was clasped about his middle. It was long, and wound about him like a tail; and it was made (for Scrooge observed it closely) of cash-boxes, keys, padlocks, ledgers, deeds and heavy purses wrought in steel. His body was transparent; so that Scrooge, observing him, and looking through his waistcoat, could see the two buttons on his coat behind. (17)

There is the spectacle of masque here, with the elaborate "costume" of Marley. His transparency and the chain are both symbolic, as the narrative later makes clear. At the same time, however, he is Jacob Marley, no allegorical figure, but a particular man with a pigtail and tassels on his boots, which are not symbolic but are merely part of the identity of a specific individual. Moreover, the symbolism in his appearance derives from no mythological or traditional sources. The ledgers and cash-boxes are, on the contrary, the very sorts of mundane accoutrements of everyday life, of "movable objects in the physical world" so important in establishing the "solidity of setting" (Watt 29) characteristic of the novel form. Dickens's purpose is too serious ever to abandon himself totally to the world of masque; and from the symbolism here emerge some of the most serious and urgent points in the book about man's conduct in the real world; later, equally, when the spirits show Scrooge various tableaux, they are not of allegorical figures or scenes, but ones from the real world, miners in their homes, or sailors on board ship. And in the using the elements of masque for such serious ends, Dickens forgets as irrelevant the essentially frivolous foundation of the masque, its complimentary purpose.

The masque as a festive form associated particularly with Christmas provides an apt basis for the sort of work Dickens wants to produce; and the adoption of elements of masque enables him to resolve a number of formal problems in writing this short work. The hybrid of masque and novel that results makes it possible to fulfill his intention of presenting a serious social message in a form in keeping with "the good-humour of the season" (xiv) to which he refers in his Preface.

Notes

1. On the masque genre, see Chambers (1: chs. 5–6), Welford and Orgel.

3. See letters to Miss Burdett Coutts, 28 February 1843 (Tillotson 447) and to Clarkson Stanfield, 5 May 1843 (Tillotson 483).

4. *The Examiner*, 4 March 1843, rpt. in Matz 99–103. Dickens possessed the text of *Comus* in the critical edition of Milton's works edited by Egerton Brydges (Tillotson 717).

5. Scrooge's position in relation to the masque is complex. He is at once a spectator and, from the reader's point of view, a participant. In this, Dickens is perhaps taking his cue from the tradition by which spectators of masques eventually became part of it by joining in the dancing at the end, taking further the "intimacy and not . . . detachment, in the relation between performers and spectators" (Chambers 195) characteristic of the form. See also Orgel's gloss on comments by the theologian John Smith relating to how the masque "attempted from the beginning to breach the barrier between spectators and actors, so that in effect the viewer became part of the spectacle . . . in a sense what the spectator watched he ultimately became" (Orgel 6–7); and, for instance, his account of a masque presented in 1501 for Katherine of Aragon in which "She does not take part in the disguising itself, but she is the central figure. In a sense she watches herself; she is both actor and spectator, and to a certain extent the boundary between stage and audience has been removed" (Orgel 26).

Works Cited

Chambers, E. K. *The Elizabethan Stage*. Oxford: Clarendon, 1923. 4 vols.

Collier, J. P. *The History of English Dramatic Poetry To the Time of Shakespeare And Annals of the Stage To the Restoration*. London: John Murray, 1831. 3 vols.

Dickens, Charles. *A Christmas Carol. Christmas Books*. Oxford Illustrated Dickens. Oxford: Oxford UP, 1954.

D'Israeli, Isaac. *Curiosities of Literature*. 1823–24. Ed. B. Disraeli. London: Frederick Warne, 1849. 3 vols.

House, Madeline, Graham Storey and Kathleen Tillotson, eds. *The Letters of Charles Dickens*. Oxford: Oxford UP, 1974.

Matz, B. W., ed. Miscellaneous Papers from 'The Morning Chronicle', 'The Daily News', 'The Examiner', 'Household Words', 'All the Year Round', Etc. Vol. 35 of *The Works of Charles Dickens*. Gadshill Edition. London: Chapman and Hall, 1914.

Orgel, Stephen. *The Jonsonian Masque*. Cambridge: Harvard UP, 1965.

Stonehouse, J. H., ed. *Reprints of the Catalogues of the Literature of Charles Dickens and William Thackeray*. London: Piccadilly Fountain P, 1935.

Tillotson, Kathleen, ed. *The Letters of Charles Dickens*. Oxford: Oxford UP, 1977.

Watt, Ian. *The Rise of the Novel*. 1957. Harmondsworth: Peregrine, 1983.

Welsford, Enid. *The Court Masque: A Study in the Relationship between Poetry and the Revels*. Cambridge: Cambridge UP, 1927.

Geoffrey Rowell Examines the Evolution of Christian Christmas

There is no doubt that *A Christmas Carol* is first and foremost a story concerned with the Christian gospel of liberation by the grace of God, and with incarnational religion which refuses to drive a wedge between the world of spirit and the world of matter. Both the Christmas dinners and the Christmas dinner-carriers are blessed; the cornucopia of Christmas food and feasting reflects both the goodness of creation and the joy of heaven. It is a significant sign of a shift in theological emphasis in the nineteenth century from a stress on the Atonement to a stress on the Incarnation, a stress which found outward and visible form in the sacramentalism of the Oxford Movement, the development of richer and more symbolic forms of worship, the building of neo-Gothic churches, and the revival and increasing centrality of the keeping of Christmas itself as a Christian festival.

At the time of the English Reformation the celebration of Christmas was retained, along with other holy days, but a strong Calvinist and Puritan theology argued that only what was explicitly commanded in Scripture was normative for Christian worship. The Christian Passover of Good Friday-Easter was the chief and most ancient of Christian festivals. Christmas only became generally celebrated in the fourth century, with the Constantinian recognition of Christianity, and the date on which it was observed, December 25th, was thought to have been chosen as a Christian counter-blast to the pagan festival of *Natali Sol Invicti*, the birthday of the unconquered Sun. When the Westminster *Directory* was substituted for the Prayer Book under the Commonwealth Christmas was abolished. The rubric stated: 'there is no day commanded in scripture to be kept holy under the gospel, but the Lord's Day, which is the Christian Sabbath', therefore 'festival-days, vulgarly called holy-days, having no warrant in the word of God, are not to be continued'.

The abolition of Christmas was by no means universally accepted. There was a report, for instance, in 1647 of a disorder at Canterbury:

> The Major endeavouring the Execution of the Ordinance for abolishing holydays was much abused by the rude multitude, had his head broken, and was dragged up and down, till he got into a house for his safety . . . Like insurrections were in several other places of the Kingdom.

The restoration of Charles II brought with it the restoration of Anglicanism, and so Christmas was restored. Pepys noted that on the first Christmas kept after the Restoration his pew was decked with the traditional rosemary and bay. At the beginning of the eighteenth century an article in the *Spectator* noted that:

> The church, as it is now equipt, looks more like a Greenhouse than a place of Worship: the middle Isle (*sic*) is a very pretty shady Walk, and the Pews look like so many Arbours of each side of it. The Pulpit itself has such Clusters of ivy, Holly, and Rosemary about it, that a light Fellow in our Pew took occasion to say, that the Congregation heard the Word out of a Bush, like Moses.

. . . Although Christmas was a time of festivity its church celebration in the nineteenth century owed much to the Oxford Movement. A significant feature of the concerns of the Tractarians was the revival and enrichment of the Prayer Book forms of service, and a proper observance of the seasons and festivals of the church calendar. It was no accident that John Keble's influential book of poems of 1827[,] entitled *The Christian Year*, provid[ed] verses and meditations on the Prayer Book services and on the Sundays and holy days observed by the Church of England. At St Saviour's, the church built by Dr Pusey in the slums of Leeds, a midnight Eucharist was celebrated on Christmas Eve in contrast to Leeds Parish Church where W.F. Hook had begun a midnight Eucharist on New Year's Eve, as an Anglican response to Methodist watch-night services. J.H. Pollen, who served as a curate in the parish, wrote of the St Saviour's Christmas in 1849. The church was decked with boughs, banners and flowers:

> Large brass candelabra were placed before the altar full of lights; three tapers were put in the place of one in the sconces of the chancel; red hangings on the walls, a rich carpet on the floor, flowers on the altar screen, a white embroidered altar frontal.

. . . What began as part of the Catholic revival in the Church of England spread to other sections of Anglicanism, and indeed to other churches. In 1887 John Hunter, a notable Church of England minister in Glasgow pioneered the keeping of Christmas Day in the kirk. In 1875 a clerical journalist, the Reverend C.M. Davies, whose collected articles on the London religious scene are invaluable vignettes of church life, noted that Christmas decorations in churches and special Christmas observances were no longer a party badge of High Churchmanship. Davies managed to visit twenty-seven churches on Christmas Day that year and noted a host of fascinating details. At St Paul's, Hammersmith, he found a splendid cross of white feathers on the pulpit, with the word 'Alleluia' on a crimson scroll. The texts on the windows were made out of tapioca. St Philip's, Earl's Court, was adorned with Christmas shrubs: 'holly, laurestina, ivy and box'. St Matthias, West Brompton, boasted ten vases of white flowers and nearly a hundred candles on the Holy Table. 'Potted hothouse flowers bedecked the altar steps, and the services were of the most ornate description'. White azaleas and camellias all but engulfed the altar at St Peter's, Kennington Park. . . . St Saviour's [also] boasted a Christmas tree. This new addition to the English Christmas was German in origin and Prince Albert has usually been credited with its introduction to England. It provided the title of the first of Dickens' Christmas Stories which appeared in *Household Words* in 1850. . . . Dickens uses the Christmas Tree as a kind of medieval memory system tracing the associations of Christmas down the branches of the tree. As the Waits' music sounds from the street, he links the powerful images of the Christmas story, with the presents of childhood. In the light of grace 'all common things become uncommon, and enchanted to me. All lamps are wonderful all rings are talismans. Common flowerpots are full of treasure'. There is the echo of the same theme of transfiguration and conversion that is so central to *A Christmas Carol*.

That Dickens chose to call his story of Scrooge's Christmas conversion *A Christmas CAROL*, is a reminder of the musical transformation of Christmas in the nineteenth century. That the story should have ghosts as a central feature is a reminder of the mid-Victorian interest in the paranormal. The most English Christmas service, the Festival of Nine Lessons and Carols, was a nineteenth-century creation, being devised by Archbishop Benson when he was bishop of the newly established see of Truro for use on Christmas Eve 1880. Although the church of the early centuries and the medieval church had employed a rival hymnody, at the Reformation the old Latin hymns were not replaced by English ones. The only hymns commonly sung were metrical versions of the psalms. Carols were originally songs of joy accompanied by a dance. The word itself comes from the Italian, *carola*, meaning 'a ring dance'. . . . Dickens' *A Christmas Carol* both reflected and contributed to the Victorian revival of Christmas. In 1844 William John Butler, soon to begin a thirty-four year model incumbency at Wantage, wrote to his parishioners near Ware in Hertfordshire:

> The people here seem hardly to feel Christmas Day. I observed that they wore their working-day clothes, and a very scanty attendance at church in proportion to that on Sundays. This seems to be the case very generally throughout the country. The people have utterly lost sight of the great Christian feasts, and with them the knowledge of the mighty events they celebrated. The Popish ways may all be very bad, but at least they teach something of the grounds of our faith and salvation. The religion of the English peasant is confined to generalities.

Butler was a keen observer (his Wantage parish diaries provide one of the fullest accounts of parochial ministry in the nineteenth century) and his comments are probably accurate. In the course of the century, under the influence of the Oxford Movement's concern for the better observance of Christian festivals, Christmas became more and more prominent. By the later part of the century cathedrals provided special services and musical events, and might have revived ancient special charities for the poor—though we must not forget the problems for large parish-church cathedrals like Manchester, which on one Christmas Day had no less than eighty couples coming to be married (the signing of the registers lasted until four in the afternoon).

The popularity of Dickens' *A Christmas Carol* played a significant part in the changing consciousness of Christmas and the way in which it was celebrated. The popularity of his public readings of the story is an indication of how much it resonated with the contemporary mood, and contributed to the increasing place of the Christmas celebration in both secular and religious ways that was firmly established by the end of the nineteenth century.

John Bowen Offers Some Thoughts on "Marley was dead: to begin with."

A Christmas Carol starts with the ambiguous words, 'Marley was dead: to begin with.'[1] Like many storytellers, Dickens begins with what appears at first to be a simple and unequivocal death, but as so often in his work there is no simple end to the life, or beginning to the story, for, as Scrooge and we learn, Jacob Marley will not stay dead. He returns to tell Scrooge to change his life, bringing with him three Christmas Spirits, festive and demanding in equal measure. Scrooge is made to visit his own grave, to appear at his own wake as it were, an event which is also his awakening. Dickens's fiction is fascinated by what is dead but will not lie down, in things or people or people-things who cross or trouble the boundaries between what was, what is, and what may be living. The novels are full of living people thought to be dead, inanimate objects made animate, human beings who become things before our eyes, and ghosts, spirits, and spectres of all kinds. The books are saturated with what Freud will later call the 'uncanny', in which the most unfamiliar event or presence will turn out to be our most familiar and disturbing acquaintance.[2] This is not simply one theme in Dickens's work, one strand in the tapestry. On the contrary, Jacob Marley's condition—being dead, but only to begin with—may be the necessary condition of all themes and all interpretation, all writing and reading of fiction, a matter of ghosts and their kin, of people or things like Scrooge, Marley, and ourselves that are dead and not dead at the same time. At important moments, Dickens's narrators encourage the reader to see the whole business of creating fictions and fictional characters as a matter of conjuring and living with ghosts, of believing-and-not-believing in the existence of Sam Weller, Sim Tappertit, Mrs Gamp, and their imaginary friends. Indeed, the novels will often stage scenes of mourning in their prefaces and conclusions for their own characters, or rather for their ghosts, which is all they ever are. And we as readers will often experience the emotion of knowing or caring more for someone who never existed, in a place and time that never were, than for those we believe to be alive around us every day. This is the perfectly normal and utterly strange effect of that activity we call reading fiction, or reading Dickens's fiction at least.

The writing of criticism shares in these effects, in its desire to conjure up its own pale ghosts: ghosts of other critics ('as Marcus has argued . . . '), ghosts of the author ('Dickens is here showing . . . '), ghosts of the work ('*Martin Chuzzlewit* is . . . ') and ghosts of you, 'the reader', who feels, knows, and intuits so much, as we tell you. These 'ghost effects' of criticism are not merely one theme among many but a condition of the criticism of fiction. And as the ghost of Marley does not come alone, or simply to disturb or question Scrooge, but obliges him to witness the poverty and exploitation of the working people and the abject poor who surround him and who suffer by his deeds, so all Dickens's fiction bears with it ethical demands upon its readers. Perhaps the best-known painting of Dickens—R. W. Buss's *Dickens's Dream*—is of the writer asleep in a chair, surrounded, haunted as it were, by his creations. In his childhood Dickens was already, he tells us, a 'strange little apparition', already haunting and haunted.[3] Many of his later critics, even the most robustly pragmatic, will find themselves reaching at key moments for the word 'haunt' or one of its derivatives.[4] Dickens will often think of dreams and other psychological processes as forms of haunting by both the living and the dead, and, as Marx will a little later in the century, think of history and historical fiction as complex and multiple hauntings and doublings of the past by the present and the present by the past.[5] As I begin now to write of 'Dickens', I seek to conjure a ghost in and from the traces of language that surround me in the name of an ethical demand and a history which has as yet no name. Like Scrooge, I am certain that Dickens is dead: to begin with.

Notes

1. Charles Dickens, *A Christmas Carol*, in *The Christmas Books Volume One*, ed. Michael Slater (Harmondsworth: Penguin, 1971), 45.

2. Sigmund Freud, 'The Uncanny' in *The Pelican Freud Library Volume 14: Art and Literature* (Harmondsworth: Penguin, 1985), 335–76.

3. John Forster, *The Life of Charles Dickens*, ed. A. J. Hoppé (London: Dent, 1966), I, 23.

4. Angus Wilson, 'Charles Dickens: A Haunting', in George H. Ford and Lauriat Lane Jr (eds), *The Dickens Critics* (Ithaca: Cornell University Press, 1961), 374–86; Malcolm Andrews, Introduction to Charles Dickens, *The Old Curiosity Shop* (Harmondsworth: Penguin, 1972), 11; Peter Ackroyd, *Dickens* (London: Sinclair Stevenson, 1990), 18, 34.

5. Karl Marx, 'The Eighteenth Brumaire of Louis Bonaparte', in David Fernbach (ed.), *Journeys from Exile* (Harmondsworth: Penguin, 1971), 143–249; Jacques Derrida, *Specters of Marx: The State of the Debt, the Work of Mourning, and the New International* (London: Routledge, 1994)

STEPHEN BERTMAN COMPARES *CAROL* AND DANTE'S *DIVINE COMEDY*

Charles Dickens's *A Christmas Carol* (1843), perhaps the most endearing work of English literature, may owe an inspirational debt to one of Italian literature's most cherished works, Dante's *Divine Comedy* (c. 1300). Although more than half a millennium separates the composition of these seemingly disparate stories, the two works exhibit striking similarities in both form and content.

In structural terms, both works are chronologically framed by key Christian holidays: *The Divine Comedy* starts on Good Friday and ends on Easter Sunday, while *A Christmas Carol* commences on Christmas Eve and culminates on Christmas Day. The main divisions of *The Divine Comedy* are three—Inferno, Purgatory, and Paradise—while *A Christmas Carol* likewise exhibits a tripartite structure marked by the visitations of three ghosts who represent past, present, and future.[1] These phantoms serve as spiritual guides for Scrooge on his enlightening trip through time, not unlike the way the souls of Virgil (in the Inferno and Purgatory), then Beatrice (in Purgatory and Paradise), and lastly St. Bernard (in the final stages of Paradise) sequentially lead Dante on his journey of divine revelation.

Deliberately dedicated to religious themes, both stories encourage us to rise above selfishness in order that we may lead a Christian life and thereby attain personal salvation. Though *The Divine Comedy* is crowded with a multitude of sinners, its plot tracks the spiritual trajectory of a single flawed human being, Dante himself. Similarly, the narrative line of *A Christmas Carol* follows the spiritual progression of another flawed individual, Ebenezer Scrooge. The soul-wrenching experience of each protagonist begins in darkness and is described as a waking dream. Each work then illustrates a litany of sins of commission and omission, depicting instances of cruelty inflicted on others or opportunities for compassion tragically lost. Each "traveler," Dante and Scrooge, finally arises from his dream-like state to a new vision of life's glorious possibilities.

As *A Christmas Carol* draws to a close (end of Stave IV), Ebenezer Scrooge, inspired by the lessons he has learned from the ghosts of Christmas Past, Christmas Present, and Christmas Yet To Come, vows to lead a changed life. "I will honour Christmas in my heart, and try to keep it all the year," he proclaims. "I will live in the Past, the Present, and the Future. The Spirits of all Three shall strive within me. I will not shut out the lessons that they teach." In a strikingly similar manner, as the *Divine Comedy* draws to a close (Paradise, Canto XXXIII), Dante has a mystical vision in which he sees three concentric circles in Heaven. These luminous celestial circles symbolize a holy trinity of time. "O eternal light!" Dante proclaims. "Sole in thyself that dwell'st; and of thyself / Sole understood, past, present, and to come" (trans. Cary). Except for the addition of the word "yet" in "*Yet* To Come," the symbolic names Dickens gave to his three spirits parallel this nineteenth century English translation of Dante's words.

There are, of course, differences in the ways the two stories are told: *The Divine Comedy* is poetically composed in the first person, while *A Christmas Carol* is narrated in third-person prose. Furthermore, in the Inferno it is the particular sins of others rather than Dante's own that are graphically catalogued. In addition, Dante's tale is more psychologically complex: the poet initially describes himself as lost in a dark forest where his path is blocked by three menacing beasts allegorically representing malice and fraud; violence and ambition; and incontinence; whereas Dickens more simply presents the tale of a man who cared only for monetary gain.

Dante would have consigned Scrooge to the Fourth Circle of his multi-level Hell, a place where misers like Scrooge were perpetually punished by pushing heavy weights that symbolized the burden of materialism. To Dante, however, the greatest sin of all was not greed but the betrayal of love, and the greatest sinner Satan who, in rebelling against God, had betrayed His love. Consequently, Satan was sentenced to the Ninth Circle, the deepest part of Hell. There he was tortured by being frozen in ice up to his waist and whipped by freezing winds generated by his own flapping wings. In Dante's view, the punishment must fit the crime: because Satan had been cold-hearted in the extreme, he had to suffer the extremities of cold rather than fiery heat.[2]

Dickens's physical description of cold-hearted Scrooge parallels Dante's physical description of Satan. Both characters, moreover, are introduced to the reader in chilling settings: Scrooge in a London seized by "piercing, searching, biting cold," and Satan in a Hellish landscape gripped by ice. Here, for example, is Dante's portrait of Satan from the English translation by Henry Francis Cary, the translation of the Inferno with which Dickens would probably have been most familiar.[3]

> *That emperor, who sways*
> *The realm of sorrow, at mid breast from th' ice*
> *Stood forth. Oh what a sight!*
> *How passing strange it seem'd, when I did spy*
> *Upon his head three faces: one in front.*
> *Of hue vermillion, th' other two with this*
> *Midway each shoulder join'd and at the crest;*
> *The right 'twixt wan and yellow seem'd; the left*
> *To look on, such as come from whence old Nile*
> *Stoops to the lowlands. Under each shot forth*
> *Two mighty wings, and these*
> *He flapp'd i' th' air, that from him issued still*
> *Three winds, wherewith Cocytus to its depth*
> *Was frozen. At six eyes he wept: the tears*
> *Adown three chins distill'd with bloody foam.*
> (Canto XXXIV.35–50)

While Dante's "chilling" description of Satan comes at the end of the Inferno, Dickens's comparably "chilling" description of Scrooge comes at the *Carol*'s start.

> The cold within him froze his old features, nipped his pointed nose, shriveled his cheek, stiffened his gait; made his eyes red, his thin lips blue and spoke out shrewdly in his grating voice. A frosty rime was on his head, and on his eyebrows, and his wiry chin. He carried his own

> low temperature always about with him; he iced his office in the dogdays; and didn't thaw it one degree at Christmas. . . . No wind that blew was bitterer than he, no falling snow was more intent upon its purpose, no pelting rain less open to entreaty. (Stave 1)

Scrooge is explicitly described by Dickens as a "sinner," and his sin, we eventually learn, was not simply that he was greedy, but that he—like Satan—had rejected the love that others (his nephew Fred and his sweetheart Belle) had offered him. The main difference between the two protagonists is that Dante's Satan was eternally damned, whereas, thanks to Dickens, Scrooge's soul could qualify for salvation.[4]

Did Dickens model *A Christmas Carol* on *The Divine Comedy* deliberately or are the parallels we have noted the result of mere coincidence? Does any evidence exist that Dickens was sufficiently familiar with *The Divine Comedy* to be influenced, even on a subconscious level, by its form and content when he set out to write *A Christmas Carol*? . . . If indeed Dickens was familiar with *The Divine Comedy*, by what means did he become acquainted with it? Though we cannot offer a definitive answer to this question, some possibilities merit consideration. Three years before Dickens wrote *A Christmas Carol*, Thomas Carlyle published *Heroes, Hero-Worship, and the Heroic in History* (1840), in which he described *The Divine Comedy* as "the most remarkable of all modern books" (80). The poem, Carlyle declared, radiated with a quality of "infinite pity" that was nevertheless tempered by a sense of justice (84). Influenced by his friend's high regard for Dante's artistry and morality, Dickens may have been induced to read Dante's work, had he not already done so, especially since it was available in Cary's "modern" English translation, one that had been warmly recommended in a lecture by Coleridge at the Royal Institution.[7] As a literary man curious about the human condition and one committed to the cause of social reform, Dickens might have been particularly fascinated by the Inferno's depiction of man's inhumanity to man and its theme of crime and punishment. In addition, as a believer in the power of education to transform people's lives,

Dickens would have been sympathetic to *The Divine Comedy*'s emphasis upon the possibility of spiritual redemption.

Speaking of Dante's Purgatory, Carlyle had declared, "There is no book so moral as this, the very essence of Christianity. . . . For life is but a series of errors made good again by repentance" (Axson 241, quoting Carlyle). All these ideas may have played a role in the composition of *A Christmas Carol*. . . . Near the end of his life, Dickens would return to an inferno, but in part one of his own creation. Two decades and more had passed since 1843 when he had excitedly "walked about the black streets of London" for hours on end, weeping and laughing and weeping again as he happily composed the *Carol* in his head (*Letters* 4: 2). Now in 1865, troubled by marital separation and the notoriety of an affair, depressed by the death of friends, and exhausted from the effort his public readings entailed, he could see only the blackness of those same streets as he contemplated *Our Mutual Friend*, the last novel he would ever complete. In this novel, as Earle Davis writes in a chapter called "Inferno," an epithet he also gives to the novel, Dickens sees London and "the Age of Victoria" wallowing "in Hell".

> From Parliament to wealthy mansions to filthy business houses to narrow streets to slums, in every part of London he saw mankind straining and struggling over a dung heap to produce money or whatever could be measured in pounds and shillings". (Davis 266)

Near the end of Dickens's life, Ebenezer Scrooge—the original Scrooge—had returned with a vengeance to haunt him.

Notes

1. The use of "Staves"—the stanzas of a song—for the *Carol*'s divisions reinforces its link with music and perhaps echoes Dante's division of *The Divine Comedy* into cantos (Italian for "songs").

2. Contrast this with Milton's description of a fiery Hell in *Paradise Lost* (1. 61–63): "A dungeon horrible, on all sides round, / As one great furnace flamed; yet from those flames/ No light; but rather darkness visible."

3. Cary's translation of the *Inferno* was originally published in 1805, followed by his translation of the complete *Divine Comedy* in 1814.

4. The permanence of damnation for the unrepentant and the availability of salvation for the contrite are illustrated in the two poems by images of gateways associated with inscriptions. Near the beginning of the *Inferno* (Canto III), Dante and Virgil pass through a portal on which is fatefully inscribed, "All hope abandon, ye who enter here" (trans. Cary). Near the end of *A Christmas Carol*, Scrooge and the Ghost of Christmas Yet To Come pass through the gate of a churchyard where Scrooge sees a gravestone inscribed with his own name, a horrifying sight that intensifies his yearning for repentance.

7. In the 1819 preface to an edition of his translation, Cary expressed his appreciation to Coleridge for "the prompt and strenuous exertions of that Gentleman in recommending the book to public notice." For the venue of Coleridge's speech, see Cary (1910) 439.

Works Cited

Axson, Stockton. "Dante and English Literature." *Dante Sexcentenary Lectures* (Rice Univ. Studies, Vol. 8, No. 2, Ch. 7). Houston, TX: Rice Univ., 1921.

Blunden, Edmund. *Leigh Hunt and His Circle*. New York & London: Harper, 1930.

Boyd, Henry. *A Translation of the Inferno of Dante Alighieri, in English Verse, with Historical Notes, and the Life of Dante. To Which Is Added, a Specimen of a New Translation of the Orlando Furioso of Ariosto*. London: C. Dilly, 1785;

———. *The Divina Commedia of Dante Alighieri: Consisting of the Inferno—Purgatorio—and Paradiso Translated into English Verse, with Preliminary Essays, Notes, and Illustrations*. London: T. Cadell jun. and W. Davies, 1802.

Carlyle, Thomas. *Heroes and Hero-Worship and the Heroic in History*. New York: Wiley & Halsted, 1859.

Cary, Henry. "Henry Francis Cary." *Encyclopedia Britannica*. 11th ed. New York: Encyclopedia Britannica, 1910. Vol. 5: 438–39.

Cary, Henry Francis, trans. *The Inferno*. 2 vols. London: James Carpenter, 1805–1806.

———. *The Vision, or Hell, Purgatory, and Paradise, of Dante*. 3 vols. London: J. Barfield; Taylor & Hessey, 1814.

Davis, Earle. *The Flint and the Flame: The Artistry of Charles Dickens*. Columbia, MO: U of Missouri P, 1963.

Dickens, Charles. *The Letters of Charles Dickens*. Ed. Graham Storey, *et al*. 12 vols. Oxford: Oxford UP, 1965–2002.

Flaxman, John. *The Illustrations for Dante's Divine Comedy*. Ed. Francesca Salvadori. London: Royal Academy of Arts, 2005.

Fontana, Ernest. "Metaphoric Mules: Dickens's Tom Gradgrind and Dante's Vanni Fucci." *The Victorian Newsletter* 109 (Spring 2006) 24–25.

Gates, Eleanor M. Ed. *Leigh Hunt: A Life in Letters*. Essex, CT: Falls River Publications, 1998.
Hunt, Leigh. *The Autobiography of Leigh Hunt*. Ed. J. E. Morpurgo. London: Cresset Press, 1949.
Stonehouse, J.H. Ed. *Catalogue of the Library of Charles Dickens from Gadshill; Catalogue of His Pictures and Objects of Art*. London: Piccadilly Fountain Press, 1935.

Les Standiford on *A Christmas Carol* as Dickens's Social Gospel

In summary, *A Christmas Carol* is a bald-faced parable that underscores Dickens's enduring themes: the deleterious effects of ignorance and want, the necessity for charity, the benefits of goodwill, family unity, and the need for celebration of the life force, including the pleasures of good food and drink, and good company. And, admittedly, Dickens is in some ways repeating concepts that he had put in print before.

But that aside, the accomplishment of this slender story, which more than one critic has termed Dickens's "most perfect" work, is to be found in the details of its rendering. In *A Christmas Carol*, a contemptible gravedigger is replaced by the much more estimable figure of a wealthy businessman. Ebenezer Scrooge is no castoff drunk, but the very emblem of economic achievement. And in place of specious advice to parents who might well want to grieve a lost child at Christmastime, he offers but a chilling vision of the Cratchit family's life without Tiny Tim, then hurries to bring that crippled child back to life again.

Furthermore, the ghosts who assail him are not vaguely drawn creatures from familiar myths. The tripartite Spirits of Christmas, preceded by the shade of Scrooge's dead partner, are as originally conceived as they are powerful in their detailed, quasi-human form. Marley appears looking very nearly as he had in life, save for the fact that "His body was transparent; so that Scrooge, observing him, and looking through his waistcoat, could see the two buttons on his coat behind. . . . [Scrooge] felt the chilling influence of its death-cold eyes; and marked the very texture of the folded kerchief bound about its head and chin, which wrapper he had not observed before."

Lest all this frightfulness open the artist to the charge of melodrama, however, Dickens slips in a typically caustic aside: "Scrooge had often heard it said that Marley had no bowels, but he had never believed it until now."

It is the sort of wit that creeps in throughout, allowing the cynical reader to proceed contentedly through the story alongside the sentimentalist. (It is not surprising, then, that one of the more enjoyable modern interpretations of the tale is performed by the comedian Jonathan Winters, master of the cutting jibe.)

And while only the hardest hearts fail to be moved along with Scrooge by the plight of the Cratchit family and the stiff-upper-lippedness of Tiny Tim, there are also moments in the text when Dickens's powers distinguish him as much as a stylist as he is a master dramatist.

Of the vast, echoing staircase in Scrooge's dimly lit town home, the narrator says, "You may talk vaguely about driving a coach-and-six up a good old flight of stairs, or through a bad young Act of Parliament; but I mean to say you might have got a hearse up that staircase, and taken it broadwise, with the splinter-bar towards the wall and the door toward the ballustrades: and done it easy. There was plenty of width for that, and room to spare; which is perhaps the reason why Scrooge thought he saw a locomotive hearse going on before him in the gloom."

The cadences, the detail, the wry humor, and the ease with which the narrator shifts from what is real to what is not—these are elements that are sometimes unrevealed to modern audiences who know *A Christmas Carol* only from dramatic adaptations, where the author's descriptive voice is replaced by a camera or by a set designer's vision. But this quality of writing contributes as much to the book's ability to work its magic upon readers as do any number of fine and noble sentiments. In such details lie the reasons why Ebenezer Scrooge and his preposterous self-centeredness would live on through history, and why Gabriel Grub, cut from the same thematic bolt of cloth, would not.

Joseph W. Childers Considers the Ideological Implications of an English Christmas

Dickens has been directly associated with Christmas since Ebenezer Scrooge, Bob Cratchit, and Tiny Tim made their first appearances 17 December 1843. By the time of his death in 1870, Dickens seemed to own the holiday. One of the most popular anecdotes recounted by Dickens biographers, and first recorded by Theodore Watts-Dunton, is of the Drury Lane barrow girl, who upon hearing of the author's death cried, "Dickens dead? Then will Father Christmas die too?" The extraordinary initial popularity of *A Christmas Carol* and its subsequent installation as a Christmas institution (it has never been out of print) have a great deal to do with the perception of Dickens as single-handedly saving Christmas from Victorian earnestness and the opprobrium of the "Hungry Forties." More precisely, however, Dickens did not so much "save" Christmas as exert considerable influence in recreating it, calling on cultural memories that were themselves yet more creations. . . . Humphry House was one of the first modern Dickens scholars to recognize the force and expansiveness of such a culture in Dickens's fiction; he wrote in 1942: "The Christmas spirit is not confined to the *Christmas* Books, the *Christmas* Stories, or the set descriptions of Christmas in the novels: it is present in the very attempt to hold up benevolence as a social ideal."[14] We can further see, especially in *A Christmas Carol* but in *The Chimes* as well, how Christmas struggles against competing views of social responsibility that are likewise attempting to resolve the contradictions of the Victorian everyday in the 1840s. Both of these texts take up the issue of the poor, the other nation, and the increasing gap between the lower and the upper classes. . . . For Scrooge's nephew, Fred, Christmas should help allay the material difficulties of the working classes and assuage the consciousness of a middle class that is caught up in a frenzy of production, consumption, and profit. As Fred says to Scrooge:

> "There are many things from which I might have derived good, by which I have not profited, I dare say. . . . Christmas among the rest. But I am sure I have always thought of Christmas time, when it has come round—apart from the veneration due to its sacred name and origin, if anything belonging to it can be apart from that—as a good time: a kind, forgiving, charitable, pleasant time: when men and women seem by one consent to open their shut-up hearts freely, and to think of people below them as if they really were fellow-passengers to the grave, and not another race of creatures bound on other journeys. And therefore, uncle, though it has never put a scrap of gold or silver in my pocket, I believe that it *has* done me good, and *will* do me good; and I say, God bless it!" (CC, stave 1)

Fred's speech demonstrates how emergent, residual, and dominant imperatives combine in a hodge-podge that both characterizes and undercuts Christmas. First, he bravely takes on the concept of political economy that dominates Scrooge's character, a notion that the text ties to Malthus and Bentham but that in Scrooge's hands is transformed into a philosophy of profit and misanthropy. Scrooge is the anti-Christmas, and by implication and association his legions are those political economists who so vulgarized Benthamite economic principles as to render a simplistic code of self-interest as the means by which society might best progress. Scrooge has translated a conception of his "good" into "profit" and marks no difference between the two. Christmas, however, demands that distinction be maintained, emerging as a set of practices and utterances that directly oppose the parsimony and solipsism of Scrooge's worldview. It materializes as a means by which the hardness of *laissez-faire* economics can be made softer, gentler, kinder.

At the same time, the residue of its "sacred name and origin," as Fred puts it, cannot be separated from it. Indeed, it gets re-enacted, retold, and re-interpreted repeatedly, even today.

Fred's defense also disrupts Christmas, however. Even while the holiday appears as a cultural entity at the heart of Victorian society—apparently doing battle with what Dickens no doubt would have labeled prevailing political-economic views—it is also subsumed by those views. Fred must take up the idiom of the political economists, a language of "good" and "profit," in order to define Christmas. Discursively it exists within the very culture it seeks to modify—if not to replace. The desire for a good old English Christmas is described in language that justifies a good *new* English Christmas, one that can be understood and approved by those who seem to hold sway in the English middle classes and who demand an explanation based on precisely those principles Scrooge represents. Further, Fred pointedly remarks on the temporariness of Christmas. For him, it is not something he holds in his heart all the year through, as Scrooge ultimately promises he will do. Rather, it "comes round" as a brief moment of generosity and good will in a "long calendar year." It is a time, for Fred, that may return every year, but also a time that passes and whose effects are fleeting. Finally, Christmas may indeed help the middle classes to think of those below them as fellow human beings, but the other side of that thought congratulates the middle classes first for being above and second for being able to patronize the poor. . . .

To some extent, the Christmas spirits open Scrooge's heart to the plight of others, but more to the point, they open his heart (and his eyes) to *his own* plight. Those events that cut Scrooge to the quick are the ones that specifically affect him. It is sad for Scrooge to think of the possible fate of Tiny Tim; it is hard for him to look upon Ignorance and Want; but it is utterly terrifying for him to witness his own mortality and his lying in an unkempt grave. Scrooge's approach to life is fundamentally no different after the visitations; he simply rethinks the source of his pleasure and his definition of value. To paraphrase awkwardly Mill paraphrasing Bentham, before the visits that source is pushpin; after, it is poetry. Scrooge's own interests are served by his keeping the Spirit of Christmas, and he completely internalizes the lessons of the "Christmas police," saying to the last ghost, "I will live in the Past, the Present, and the Future. The Spirits of all Three shall strive within me. I will not shut out the lessons that they teach." He then turns once again to his own headstone and exclaims, "Oh tell me I may sponge away the writing on this stone" (CC, stave 4), as though their lessons promised material, and not spiritual, immortality.[15]

Without completely abandoning an analysis of the *Carol*, I want to consider this culture of Christmas in its larger implications, including some of those that I mentioned at the beginning of this chapter. Not only do I want to insist that the version of Christmas articulated in the *Carol* is coded as English in its specific concerns: of the poor, of the Manchester school of political economy, of the traditions (real or imagined) of Christmases past. I also want to maintain that even in its early iterations, the Victorian culture of Christmas yokes Englishness to what it is now fashionable to label "liberal guilt." . . . Daniel Born points out . . . that as the century progressed, the optimism of the first generation of liberal theorists that poverty, social inequity, and coercive government could be overcome gave way to the realization that capitalist and liberal value systems make uneasy bedfellows.[17] The confidence of the earlier generation was waning by the time we get to Dickens, even early Dickens, and prescription turned to guilt. The great liberal political and social reforms of the 1830s no longer seemed capable, in the 1840s, of eradicating the problems of inequality and suffering they had been designed to address. The facts of the two nations and the hungry masses could not be explained away; it became impossible to justify the almost unspannable chasm between the lower and middle classes in the richest country in the world. In Dickens we find no suggestion of a systematic way for society to face these problems—nor should we necessarily expect to: there is no getting rid of poverty, inequity, and ill-use; there is only individual intervention, the possibility of making things spiritually and materially better for a few. . . .

Such is Scrooge's case. In a tale that quickly transforms the humanistic shortcomings of *laissez-faire* economics into an allegory, the problem of the employer who pays the exact wages fixed by supply and demand and whose primary moral failing is his lack of sympathy for the troubles of the poor is solved by transforming the individual. The result: Cratchit gets better wages and Scrooge a better temper. The masses of poor still go about poorly fed, poorly clothed, and poorly sheltered, however; and if any other Scrooges existed in England, they no doubt slept soundly on Christmas Eve. . . .

The problem that remains for the tale is that humanity and the common welfare were indeed Marley's (and now are Scrooge's) business; if the dealings of their trade are "but a drop of water in the comprehensive ocean" (CC, stave 1) of their business, what sorts of comprehensive *measures* are being taken so that business gets managed? In the *Carol* none, really, and in *The Chimes* only workhouses and prisons. At such points, the basic contradiction at the heart of the Victorian culture of the English Christmas is readily apparent: on the one hand, it insists on a muted Christian socialism that restores human sympathy and relieves spiritual and physical want; on the other, it simultaneously celebrates the individual's ability to effect at least small-scale, localized change. Also at stake is the individual himself, especially the condition of his soul, or even, as Scrooge's narrative corroborates, the individual's interiority—a specific emotional and intellectual relationship to the past and present as well as to the possibilities of the future. Scrooge's largesse is still an investment in his eternal destiny; that he also acquires pleasure from it is an accrued advantage, to be sure, but he is never freed from his guilt, his responsibility.[20] If anything, his position as the self-made, middle-class Englishman of business is inexorably linked to his guilt and makes him even *more* aware of it.[21] None of the spirits, or anyone else, ever suggests that Scrooge sell his business and give all the proceeds to the poor or even that he raise Cratchit's position by making him a partner; the way he can best attend to the needs of the lower classes is to remain a man of business and a successful one at that. He just needs to try a little tenderness. Thus,

Christmas attempts to curb the predatory aspects of capitalism, but never does away with it altogether. This, perhaps, is the gift of the English tradition of Christmas to the rest of the world, for we can see the culture of Christmas continuing to function in this way. . . .

The power of Christmas has become so formidable in our own time that it is nearly impossible to imagine it without "all the trimmings" of its Victorian heritage and the unique, sometimes grandiose, articulations of liberal guilt that surround our observance of the holiday. Whatever one's religion, in the anglicized world, Christmas has transformed into an annual assertion of a set of ideological assumptions that, at least for the season, abide without serious threat or opposition. Just as for Scrooge's nephew, it is held up as a fleeting moment of universal goodwill and tolerance, of searching out and eradicating cruelty—whether in the form of feeding hungry third-world children, commuting prisoners' sentences, or simply thinking, for a brief time, of the needs and desires of others. As Fred implies, this can a very good thing indeed. Yet the idea of "virtue as its own reward," if, in fact, it ever really existed within the culture of Christmas, has been fairly successfully siphoned out of the practices that inform contemporary versions of the holiday, replaced by impulses toward self-fulfillment and consumerism: those traits of Christmas that Dickens tries to belie, but without which it is impossible for him to discuss Christmas at all. In those instances when we identify acts of generosity and thoughtfulness that are not self-directed, we tend to undercut their substance by highlighting them in the media and proclaiming them the "true spirit" of Christmas. We typically fail to see in them one of their most significant functions: as nostalgic nods toward an imaginary time within modern memory, when Christmas was divorced from the social forces that created Mr. Chokepear and Mr. Scrooge and that continue to exert considerable pressure on our own understandings of Christmas, as the *Daily Express*'s urgent proclamations demonstrate. We have indeed inherited Dickens's version of Christmas, and all its contradictory ideological baggage with it. To try to reform it may well lead us back to the dilemmas that we see bedeviling *A Christmas Carol*. To try to understand it within its context of Christian, liberal, and nationalist ideologies may produce entirely different results.

Notes

14. Humphry House, *The Dickens World*, 53–54.

15. Cf. House's comment on Scrooge's conversion: "Scrooge does not see the Eternal behind the Temporal, a new heaven and earth: he merely sees the old earth from a slightly different angle" (*The Dickens World*, 53).

17. See Daniel Born, *The Birth of Liberal Guilt in the English Novel*, 1–17. Born identifies the emergence of liberal guilt in the fiction of the period in *Little Dorrit* and argues that it wanes during the Edwardian period. His argument rests upon the move from novelists' emphases on individual responsibility (as in *A Christmas Carol*), which he links to a culture of Christianity, to social responsibility (apparently first observable for Born in *Little Dorrit*), which he characterizes as more secular in its motivations. In contrast, I contend that "liberal guilt" is already at work as a significant social force, owing, in part, to the overdetermined effects of political economy on the shape of increasingly compelling and numerous articulations of moral responsibility by the middle classes, at least as early as the 1840s.

20. It is never entirely clear that the pleasure Scrooge receives from "keeping Christmas" throughout the year is his enjoyment of the camaraderie and humanity of the holiday or the anticipation of laying up his own "treasures in heaven."

21. Audrey Jaffe makes a similar observation regarding the readers of *A Christmas Carol*: "The story's ideological project—its attempt to link sympathy and business by incorporating a charitable impulse into its (male) readers' self-conceptions—underlies its association of charitable feeling with participation in cultural life" ("Spectacular Sympathy," 329).

Works by Charles Dickens

Sketches by Boz and *The Pickwick Papers* (1836)

Oliver Twist (1837)

Nicholas Nickleby (1838)

Sketches of Young Couples; *The Old Curiosity Shop* (1840)

Barnaby Rudge (1841)

American Notes (1842)

Martin Chuzzlewit and *A Christmas Carol* (1843)

The Chimes (1844)

The Cricket on the Hearth (1845)

Pictures from Italy and *Dombey and Son* (1846)

The Haunted Man (1848)

David Copperfield (1849)

Bleak House (1852)

Hard Times (1854)

Little Dorrit (1855)

A Tale of Two Cities (1859)

Great Expectations (1860)

Our Mutual Friend (1864)

The Mystery of Edwin Drood, unfinished (1870)

Annotated Bibliography

Andrews, Malcolm. *Charles Dickens and His Performing Selves: Dickens and the Public Readings*. Oxford and New York: Oxford University Press, 2006.

This study of Dickens focuses on his public identity and the effect on audiences of his public readings of his stories. The author laments that no recording of Dickens reading exists because he died seven years after the invention of the phonograph. There are some memories of these readings written and preserved by people who most appreciated this part of Dickens's work, but, as Andrews writes, "If only we could summon the weary man back for an encore" (viii). The book is an attempt to recreate the experience and significance of Dickens's public readings (of which *A Christmas Carol* was the most frequently performed).

Bodenheimer, Rosemarie. *Knowing Dickens*. Ithaca and London: Cornell University Press, 2007.

This study of Dickens's letters and fiction addresses the questions (said by the author to be underexamined) where is Dickens's literary imagination located, what are its sources, and why did he spend his life writing novels? The author asks: "What are the internal plots this writer carried around throughout his life, his characteristic patterns of experience, response, and counterresponse? . . . To what extent is it possible for us to know what and how Dickens knew?" (2). To begin, the author looks at evidence for the history and literature Dickens was familiar with and the extent of his travels beyond England. For other resources, she looks to family relationships, issues in contemporary England, especially the newly industrial England, and larger cultural influences such as issues of class and poverty and the insights of Freud. Most of Dickens's major works are discussed.

Bowen, John. *Other Dickens: Pickwick to Chuzzlewit*. Oxford: Oxford University Press, 2000.

Introducing his book, the author states that his study will focus on Dickens's earlier novels and other writings that have been in recent decades regarded as less accomplished and less worthy of critical attention—thus his title—than the later novels *Great Expectations*, *Bleak House*, *Hard Times*, *Little Dorrit*, and *Our Mutual Friend.* Bower points out that early readers found enjoyment and substance in *Pickwick Papers*, *Oliver Twist*, *Nicholas Nickleby*, and *Martin Chuzzlewit* and argues that scholars should examine why this is so. Specifically, Bowen reminds his readers that theories of literary criticism are continually undergoing change and that with new perspectives or a renewed look with old perspectives, the earlier writings will be found more worthy of attention.

Chesterton, G.K. *Charles Dickens: The Last of the Great Men.* New York: The Press of the Reader's Club, 1942.

As the title suggests, this volume is more tribute and high praise than literary criticism, but Chesterton, an author himself, was familiar with all the major writers up to that time, and his praise was trusted by many readers. The imperatives of the Christian faith were central in Chesterton's thinking and he approaches Dickens's life with these personal perspectives. An example occurs in the foreword where Alexander Woollcott quotes Chesterton reflecting on what Dickens was trying to convey: "that comradeship and serious joy are not interludes in our travel; but that rather our travels are interludes in comradeship and joy, which through God shall endure forever. The inn does not point to the road; the road points to the inn" (ix). A chronology and brief biography reprinted from the *Encyclopedia Britannica* are included.

Davis, Paul. *The Lives and Times of Ebenezer Scrooge.* New Haven and London: Yale University Press, 1990.

This study focuses on the origins, impact, and multiple manifestations over the decades of Dickens's *A Christmas Carol.* The author notes his own preliterate assimilation of the story of Scrooge's conversion and Tiny Tim's universal and joyful declaration. He speculates that the *Carol*'s rapid and hugely successful evolution from written story to oral performance to family read-aloud sessions makes it unlikely that anyone alive today could remain unfamiliar with Ebenezer and the story of his conversion. Even American entertainment had its own Uncle Scrooge McDuck. Each chapter presents some aspect of the story from its early inspirations, early performances, history in the United States, impact on the celebration of Christmas, and its innumerable adaptations. The volume concludes with an eleven-page section listing in chronological order (1843–1988) "some noteworthy versions" of Dickens's *A Christmas Carol*. Illustrations from several editions and scenes from several film versions are found throughout.

Gillooly, Eileen and Deirdre David, eds. *Contemporary Dickens*. Columbus: The Ohio State University Press, 2009.

The essays in this volume have in common a belief that Dickens's work can and should be read with a view to its contemporary relevance. There is even an essay that sees Dickens—who was alert to the ravages of midcentury industrialism on the environment in London and elsewhere in England—as a "green" writer. Another provides a critical perspective on Dickens's perceptive views on attitudes behind social philanthropy and charity. Other essays focus on gender and sexual questions that were obliquely addressed by Victorian thinkers and the great social issues of poverty and class differences that were addressed directly but never resolved.

Gold, Joseph. *Charles Dickens: Radical Moralist*. Minneapolis: University of Minnesota Press, 1972.

In his introduction, the author defines the moralist as artist as "someone who believes in and reveals to us our own possibilities for living more meaningfully" and the reformer as "someone who wants to see a different society appear by some means or other" (10). He believes Dickens the writer combines these different roles and examines the main writings to illustrate this belief.

Hardy, Barbara. *The Moral Art of Dickens*. London: The Athlone Press of the University of London, 1970.

The author is interested in the specifically moral aspects of Dickens's work and in clarifying the differences in moral imagination among Dickens, George Eliot, and Henry James. She dwells on what she calls the "crudity" or "conspicuousness" of Dickens's engagement with moral issues. The first half of her study discusses generalizations about Dickens's moral concerns and how these evolved during his lifetime. The second half of the study looks at specific expressions of moral concerns in four of his novels.

Jordan, John O., ed. *The Cambridge Companion to Charles Dickens*. Cambridge: Cambridge University Press, 2001.

The essays collected for this volume were written after nearly a century and a half of written commentary about Dickens's life and work, and the writer of the first essay points out that theories of understanding literary works and their authorship have gone through several major changes over the years. In addition, the editor points out in his brief preface that Dickens need no longer be made more accessible to the reader, but a need does exist to present the familiar material from some of these new perspectives. Consequently, new readers of Dickens might want to study these essays after becoming familiar with some of the more traditional criticism. A chronology is included as well as several illustrations in the essays dealing with Dickens and illustration and film.

Louttit, Chris. *Dickens's Secular Gospel: Work, Gender, and Personality*. New York and London: Routledge, 2009.

Except for the concept of God, the concept and value of work was understood to be of prominent importance in the Victorian age. The author of this volume acknowledges the omnipresence of work in Victorian daily life and also the high esteem in which it was held but challenges the idea that Dickens shared his contemporary Thomas Carlyle's promotion of work as "noble" activity. Looking closely first at letters and then at the novels, the author finds many instances in which Dickens refers to work as a kind of bondage or imprisonment. The opposite of work, namely, idleness and inactivity, are also examined.

Love, Teresa R. *Dickens and the Seven Deadly Sins*. Danville, Ill.: The Interstate Printers & Publishers, 1979.

Dickens has traditionally been studied as a writer with prominent moral concerns; this study continues that critical line but looks specifically at the Christian foundation of these moral principles. The author cites a contemporary upsurge of interest in Dickens's work as a sign that his larger, essentially artistic issues are being recognized. Before this renewal of interest, Dickens tended to be regarded as a mere comic artist, an entertainer, or as an excessively didactic writer—in line with the preoccupations of the Victorian age. The author gives a chapter each to the sins of avarice, gluttony, pride, sloth, envy and anger, and lust and one chapter to the comingling of all sins as dramatized in *Bleak House*. This study is both interesting and accessible for new students of Dickens's work.

Morris, Pam. *Dickens's Class Consciousness: A Marginal View*. New York: St. Martin's Press, 1991.

The author's approach to Dickens's writing is rooted in ideological and psychoanalytic considerations. She points out that, although Dickens was not born into the working class of his time, the early experiences of his father's imprisonment and his childhood stint as a factory laborer not only made him acutely aware of the physical consequences of poverty but more importantly caused him to feel marginalized in society. The author argues that Dickens held a complex attitude toward both his central characters as well as those living desperately on society's margins. Several of the novels are discussed from this perspective.

Paroissien, David, ed. *A Companion to Charles Dickens*. Malden, Mass., Oxford, England, and Victoria, Australia: Blackwell Publishing, 2008.

To enhance the understanding and enjoyment of Dickens's work, the editor has assembled thirty-six essays in five parts, each devoted to the illumination of some aspect of Dickens studies: biographical facts and insights, cultural and literary contexts, historical contexts, new readings of the works themselves, and reputation and influence. One essay discusses the illustrations that usually accompanied Dickens's publications and offers many samples of these.

Standiford, Les. *The Man Who Invented Christmas: How Charles Dickens's "A Christmas Carol" Rescued His Career and Revived Our Holiday Spirits*. New York: Crown Publishers, 2008.

This biographical study of Dickens focuses mainly on those aspects of his life that would later appear to have influenced his embracing and reviving the tradition of Christmas as it is popularly celebrated today in this country and England. The author includes early passages from the writer's letters and recollected conversations that express his full appreciation of Christmas and his hope for restoring the generosity, goodwill, and festivity that had gone in and out of favor over centuries of observation. The book is mainly about the creation of *A Christmas Carol* and its evolution in popular culture and performance.

Vogel, Jane. *Allegory in Dickens*. Tuscaloosa: University of Alabama Press, 1977.

This study of Dickens focuses on the writer as a Christian and allegorical novelist. The author anticipates that once the Christian framework for the novels has been established, more detailed studies of each work will follow. For this volume, she intends to provide an overview.

Wilson, Edmund. *The Triple Thinkers & The Wound and the Bow: A Combined Volume*. Boston: Northeastern University Press, 1984.

Edmund Wilson was known for his astute insights and lucid writing about literary figures and issues. His lengthy essay on Dickens—"Dickens: The Two Scrooges"—found in *The Wound and the Bow* is an example of these talents.

Contributors

Harold Bloom is Sterling Professor of the Humanities at Yale University. Educated at Cornell and Yale universities, he is the author of more than 30 books, including *Shelley's Mythmaking* (1959), *Blake's Apocalypse* (1963), *Yeats* (1970), *The Anxiety of Influence* (1973), *A Map of Misreading* (1975), *Kabbalah and Criticism* (1975), *Agon: Toward a Theory of Revisionism* (1982), *The American Religion* (1992), *The Western Canon* (1994), *Omens of Millennium: The Gnosis of Angels, Dreams, and Resurrection* (1996), *Shakespeare: The Invention of the Human* (1998), *How to Read and Why* (2000), *Genius: A Mosaic of One Hundred Exemplary Creative Minds* (2002), *Hamlet: Poem Unlimited* (2003), *Where Shall Wisdom Be Found?* (2004), *Jesus and Yahweh: The Names Divine* (2005), and *Till I End My Song: A Gathering of Last Poems* (2010). In addition, he is the author of hundreds of articles, reviews, and editorial introductions. In 1999, Professor Bloom received the American Academy of Arts and Letters' Gold Medal for Criticism. He has also received the International Prize of Catalonia, the Alfonso Reyes Prize of Mexico, and the Hans Christian Andersen Bicentennial Prize of Denmark.

Barbara Hardy is professor emeritus at the University of London and a member of the Royal Society of Literature and the British Academy. She has written extensively on English literature, including two works on Dickens—*The Moral Art of Dickens* and *Charles Dickens: The Later Novels.*

Jane Vogel teaches in the department of English at Ithaca College.

Teresa R. Love has taught in the English department at Southern Illinois University.

Paul Davis, a professor emeritus at the University of Mexico, is the author of *The Life and Times of Ebenezer Scrooge* (1990), the

Penguin *Dickens Companion* (1999), and the *Critical Companion to Charles Dickens: A Literary Reference to his Life and Work* (2007).

Donald R. Burleson teaches at Eastern New Mexico University. In 2010, he published *The Capitalist Christmas Carol: Charles Dickens Meets Ayn Rand.*

R.D. Butterworth is the author of the essays "*A Christmas Carol* and the Masque" from *Studies in Short Fiction* and "The First New England Christmas" from *A Budget of Christmas Tales.*

Geoffrey Rowell, fellow, chaplain, and tutor in theology at Oxford University, is the author of *The Vision Glorious: Themes and Personalities of the Catholic Revival in Anglicanism* (1983).

John Bowen is a professor of nineteenth-century literature at the University of York in the United Kingdom. He is the author of *Charles Dickens: Pickwick to Chuzzlewit.*

Stephen Bertman is associated with the University of Windsor.

Les Standiford is the director of the creative writing program at Florida International University in Miami. He has written ten novels and received the Frank O'Connor Award for Short Fiction.

Joseph W. Childers, a professor in the English department at the University of California in Riverside, is well known for his writing on Victorian literature and culture. He co-edited *Victorian Prism: Refractions of the Crystal Palace* (2007) and the forthcoming *Sublime Economy: Intersections of Aesthetic and Economics.*

Acknowledgments

Barbara Hardy, "The Change of Heart (1)." From *The Moral Art of Dickens*, pp. 27, 30–31, 34–37. Published by the Athlone Press. Copyright © Barbara Hardy 1970.

Jane Vogel, "An Overview of Allegory in Dickens." From *Allegory in Dickens*, pp. 42–43, 70–73. Copyright © 1977 by the University of Alabama Press.

Theresa R. Love, "Avarice." From *Dickens and the Seven Deadly Sins*, pp. 39–42, 138. Copyright © 1979 by the Interstate Printers & Publishers.

Paul Davis, "Founder of the Feast," pp. 81-84, 86-87 and "The Greening of Scrooge," pp. 175–77. From *The Lives and Times of Ebenezer Scrooge*. Copyright © 1990 by Yale University.

Donald R. Burleson, "Dickens's *A Christmas Carol*." From *Explicator* 50, no. 4 (Summer 1992): 211–12. Copyright © 1992 Taylor and Francis.

R.D. Butterworth, "*A Christmas Carol* and Masque." From *Studies in Short Fiction* 30 (1993): 63–69. Copyright © 1993 by Newberry College.

Geoffrey Rowell, "Dickens and the Construction of Christmas." From *History Today* (December 1993): 19–22, 24. Copyright © 1993 *History Today*.

John Bowen, "Arbitrary and Despotic Characters." From *Other Dickens:* Pickwick *to* Chuzzlewit, pp. 1–3. Published by Oxford University Press. Copyright © John Bowen 2000.

Stephen Bertman, "Dante's Role in the Genesis of Dickens's *A Christmas Carol*." From *Dickens Quarterly* 24, no. 3 (September 2007): 167–73. Copyright © 2007 *Dickens Quarterly*.

Les Standiford, "Let Nothing Ye Dismay." From *The Man Who Invented Christmas: How Charles Dickens's A Christmas Carol Rescued His Career and Revived Our Holiday Spirits*, pp. 100–02. Published by Crown Publishers. Copyright © 2008 by Les Standiford.

Joseph W. Childers, "So, This Is Christmas." From *Contemporary Dickens*, edited by Eileen Gillooly and Deirdre David, pp. 115–19, 122–30. Copyright © 2009 by the Ohio State University.

Index